A VICTORY FOR LOVE

I0670970

Barbara Cartland

Barbara Cartland Ebooks Ltd

This edition © 2018

Copyright Cartland Promotions 1985

ISBNs

9781788670753   EPUB
9781788670760   PAPERBACK
Book design by M-Y Books
m-ybooks.co.uk

THE BARBARA CARTLAND ETERNAL COLLECTION

The Barbara Cartland Eternal Collection is the unique opportunity to collect all five hundred of the timeless beautiful romantic novels written by the world's most celebrated and enduring romantic author.

Named the Eternal Collection because Barbara's inspiring stories of pure love, just the same as love itself, the books will be published on the internet at the rate of four titles per month until all five hundred are available.

The Eternal Collection, classic pure romance available worldwide for all time .

THE LATE DAME BARBARA CARTLAND

Barbara Cartland, who sadly died in May 2000 at the grand age of ninety eight, remains one of the world's most famous romantic novelists. With worldwide sales of over one billion, her outstanding 723 books have been translated into thirty six different languages, to be enjoyed by readers of romance globally.

Writing her first book 'Jigsaw' at the age of 21, Barbara became an immediate bestseller. Building upon this initial success, she wrote continuously throughout her life, producing bestsellers for an astonishing 76 years. In addition to Barbara Cartland's legion of fans in the UK and across Europe, her books have always been immensely popular in the USA. In 1976 she achieved the unprecedented feat of having books at numbers 1 & 2 in the prestigious B. Dalton Bookseller bestsellers list.

Although she is often referred to as the 'Queen of Romance', Barbara Cartland also wrote several historical biographies, six autobiographies and numerous theatrical plays as well as books on life, love, health and cookery. Becoming one of Britain's most popular media personalities and dressed in her trademark pink, Barbara spoke on radio and television about social and political issues, as well as making many public appearances.

In 1991 she became a Dame of the Order of the British Empire for her contribution to literature and her work for humanitarian and charitable causes.

Known for her glamour, style, and vitality Barbara Cartland became a legend in her own lifetime. Best remembered for her wonderful romantic novels and loved by millions of readers worldwide, her books remain treasured for their heroic heroes, plucky heroines and traditional values. But above all, it was Barbara Cartland's overriding belief in the positive power of love to help, heal and improve the quality of life for everyone that made her truly unique.

AUTHOR'S NOTE

One of the great menaces of the War waged in Spain and France by the Duke of Wellington's Armies against Napoleon was the scavengers who stole everything they could from the dead and dying on the battlefield.

Bodies that were left for any length of time became unidentifiable when they were finally collected, either by members of their Regiments or by the nuns and others who were merciful.

This pernicious practice of stealing continued right up to my grandfather's time when he remembered seeing, after the Battle of Sedan in 1870, hundreds of letters strewn about the battlefield that had been written by men before they had been killed. They were blown by the wind after their clothing and everything they owned had been taken from them.

CHAPTER ONE
1817

Farica, walking through the wood very quietly on moss-covered paths, thought that the trees with their first summer foliage were lovelier than she had ever seen them.

She knew that in a moment or two that there would be an opening and she would see ahead of her the magnificent facade of Lyde Castle.

The Castle of the Earl of Lydbrooke had been to her a Fairy Palace that had coloured the stories her mother read to her and those she later told herself when she was always the heroine.

Today Lyde meant something definite to her personally, although she was not certain if it pleased her or not.

As she moved through the trees, looking in her green muslin gown as if she was part of them, she saw with surprise that there was a man sitting on a fallen tree trunk just ahead of her.

It was a trunk that she had intended to sit on herself to look at The Castle and she stopped, thinking it extremely annoying that there was someone else already there.

She wondered if she should retreat rather than encounter a stranger.

Just as she was feeling indecisive, she saw something glitter in his hand and a second later was aware that it was a pistol.

He lifted it a little and with a feeling of shock Farica was certain that he was going to raise it to his temple.

Without thinking that she might become involved, without considering what might be the consequences, she ran forward and in a low breathless voice asserted,

"No – you must – not do that! It's a – wicked – cowardly thing to do!"

As she spoke, she put out her hand and laid it on his arm.

He turned his face towards her obviously startled by her interference.

As she looked at him, she was aware that he was a man she had never seen before and he was also a gentleman.

For a moment they just gazed at each other.

Then she said a little incoherently as she took her hand from his arm,

"I-I am sorry – I thought you – intended to – kill yourself."

"And you considered it your duty to stop me."

His voice was low and deep and Farica blushed as she replied,

"Perhaps you think – I had no right to interfere. But life is so precious – it should not be wasted."

There was a faint twist to his lips before he replied,

"Where I have come from life was a very cheap commodity and of little value. But I am sure, where you are concerned, it is indeed very precious."

She realised that it was a compliment and blushed again.

Then she said,

"I can only apologise – but we are not used to people brandishing pistols about in this part of the country, unless, of course – they are highwaymen."

The gentleman smiled.

"And you don't think that I am one?"

"No, I am sure you are not," Farica replied. "At the same time please – put that dangerous weapon away. It frightens me."

As if the gentleman suddenly realised that he was sitting and she was standing, he rose to his feet and as he did so put his pistol into the pocket of his coat.

It was of a cheap material and not in the least fashionable and yet as he stood facing her she was still sure that in spite of his appearance he was well bred.

Then he smiled and it seemed to transform his rather thin grim face.

"I suppose I should be thanking you for your consideration of me," he said, "in what was meant, I am sure, as an act of kindness."

Farica did not answer and after a moment he added as if to himself,

"And I am very much in need of kindness at the moment."

Looking at him Farica saw that there was a long scar at the side of his square forehead and she said a little tentatively,

"I think, sir, that you have been – a soldier."

"Does it show so obviously?"

"Then you have!" Farica exclaimed. "If you have just returned from France, after perhaps in the last year being in the Army of Occupation – you must find things very strange and different in England."

"So different," the gentleman replied, "that it made you think that, being unable to face it, I intended to shoot myself."

Farica looked at him wide-eyed and he went on,

"Well, you are not very far from the truth. I do find things very different, but I am not sure what I can do about it."

"I am sorry," Farica said in a soft sympathetic voice. "I know how hard it must be for you. Papa has been desperately perturbed about the way our soldiers who fought so gallantly against Bonaparte have been disbanded without a pension and nothing is done to find them employment, which is very difficult to obtain at the moment."

The gentleman nodded his head as if this was what he had found himself and then Farica asked him,

"Will you tell me what Regiment you were in?"

To her surprise the gentleman seemed to hesitate for a moment before he replied,

"I was in the Life Guards."

"Then you fought at the Battle of Waterloo," she exclaimed breathlessly.

The gentleman nodded again and she went on,

"I have read everything I could find about that magnificent battle and how brave our soldiers were."

She gave a little sigh and murmured almost beneath her breath,

"But – a great many – died or were wounded."

"That is true."

Without being aware of what she was doing Farica walked round from behind the tree trunk and sat down on it.

"My brother was – killed in the Peninsula," she said. "He died gallantly – but I still find it hard to believe that I shall never – see him again."

The gentleman resumed his seat on the trunk beside her before he replied,

"War is cruel, not only to those who fight but to those who wait behind."

Farica gave a deep sigh.

"That is true. We waited and waited, because the first letter from Rupert's Commanding Officer never reached us and when at last we knew the truth – it almost killed Papa."

There was a little sob in her voice and her eyes were misty.

The man beside her said nothing but looked at her.

She was very small and sylph-like with a pointed face and strange eyes that turned up at the corners, giving her an elfin look.

'She is quite beautiful,' he thought to himself, 'beautiful with her hair the colour of the copper beech, every curl gold-tipped as if touched by the sunshine.'

It was a strangely haunting little face that, he told himself, a man would find it hard to forget.

Her voice was soft and musical like the wind blowing in the leaves.

With an effort Farica seemed almost to shake herself before she said,

"I should not be talking about myself but about you. Now you are back from the War, what are you going to do?"

"That is exactly the question I was asking," the gentleman replied, "and when you appeared to prevent me from committing what you called a 'cowardly act', I had not found the answer."

He smiled as he finished speaking, but Farica looked serious.

"It is going to be very very difficult for you," she said, "if you have no money and no family to look after you."

"I suppose that is the luck of the draw. I must just pray that Fate or the Gods will be kind to me, which they have been already in letting me meet you."

"Thank you," Farica said, "but I don't want you to pay me any compliments. I wish, if it is possible, to help you."

"Why?"

The question was sharp and she looked at him in surprise before she replied,

"Because you have been a soldier and because, although it may seem a strange thing to say, you have brought your problem to the same place as I have – brought mine."

"You have a problem?"

She nodded her head.

"A very big one!"

The man beside her looked at her for a long moment before he said,

"Now I am being perceptive or perhaps you would call it 'clairvoyant', but I am sure your problem concerns a man and, of course, love and marriage."

"It is not – quite like – that."

"Then marriage!"

She did not reply, but he knew that he had struck the right note.

"And you have come here," he said, as if he was thinking it out for himself, "to decide whether you should marry somebody who I am sure is important and distinguished and who has asked for your hand, but you do *not* love him."

"That is – right," Farica agreed a little breathlessly. "How could I marry any man – unless I loved him? That is what I came here – to ask myself."

Her eyes, which had a touch of green in them, were troubled and, as she looked towards Lyde Castle, vast, impressive and magnificent in the sunshine, the gentleman followed the direction of her eyes and said,

"Are you telling me that your suitor is the Earl of Lydbrooke?"

Farica gave a little cry.

"Please – you must not probe too deeply or guess at things that do not concern you. Papa would be very shocked that – I was talking so intimately with a stranger."

There was a little silence and then the gentleman said,

"I think for the moment, here in this wood, we have stepped out of time and space and away from all the conventions of life."

He paused and, as Farica looked at him wonderingly, he went on,

"You are a nymph from the woods who has a problem and I am a wise old man, a sage if you like, who will try to guide you so that you don't hurt yourself, but will find the golden path to happiness."

He spoke in a low deep voice that seemed to be characteristic of him and Farica clasped her hands together as she said,

"That is a lovely idea! I only wish I was a nymph of the woods, a real nymph, and then I could disappear into the trees and no one could find me – or make me do things I have no wish to do."

"I think by that you mean you have no wish to marry."

She twisted her long thin fingers together before she replied,

"How can I marry him when I have – only seen him two or three times? And I cannot believe – whatever Papa may say that he – loves me."

There was poignant silence for a moment.

Then the gentleman said,

"Tell me about the Earl. Before I went abroad to the War his father, I think, was living here at The Castle."

"He was a dear old man," Farica replied, "and he was kind to Papa when he bought The Priory where we live. Our other neighbours in the County, because we were newcomers, were rather inclined to – 'look down their noses' at us."

"Then what happened?" the gentleman prompted.

"The Earl asked Papa to dinner. Of course I was too young in those days to be invited, but he used to speak to me out hunting and – after he had led the way everybody accepted Papa and invited him to their houses."

Farica paused for breath.

Then she went on,

"Papa told me how worried the Earl was that his son was in the thick of the fighting. Everybody around here loved him, the Viscount, and prayed that he would come home safely."

"Are you saying that he was killed?" the gentleman asked.

Farica nodded.

"Right at the very end of the War. In fact at the Battle of Waterloo, although no one knew it for some time."

She sighed deeply before she said,

"I think that made the Earl no longer wish to go on living – and at his funeral they mourned his son with him."

Her voice was very moving and there was silence until the gentleman asked,

"But who is the new Earl who is asking for your hand in marriage?"

"He is a nephew and never came here during his uncle's lifetime – because they did not get on."

"Why was that?"

"Papa told me that it was because Fergus, that is the present Earl's name, was wildly extravagant and preferred the gaieties of London to sport in the country."

She gave him a little smile before she added,

"I am being very indiscreet and just repeating gossip when I say that the old Earl paid his nephew's debts over and over again until he told him that he would do so no more."

"And this is the man your father wishes you to marry?" the gentleman asked and the surprise in his voice was clear.

Farica looked embarrassed as she said,

"Papa is very rich and I cannot help feeling that is really the reason – why the Earl of Lydbrooke is interested in me!"

"I cannot understand how your father can consider such a marriage for you," the gentleman commented with a sharp note in his voice.

Farica made a little gesture with her hands.

"I think the truth is that Papa has always felt that despite the support he had from the old Earl, many people in the County felt that he was not really grand enough for them. He is only a second Baronet, while the people around here are utter snobs and keep talking about their ancestors as if they were all derived from Adam!"

The gentleman laughed.

"I know exactly what you mean. At the same time you must think of yourself and remember it is you who would be marrying the Earl and not your father!"

"Papa is pleased at the idea of my being the chatelaine of Lyde Castle and, as his estate marches with this one, which was, I think, originally part of it, it would seem a very sensible arrangement if the boundaries were merged."

She paused and then went on,

"You have no idea how much disagreeableness there is every year because Papa's gamebirds fly onto the Lyde estate and they say we poach theirs. The keepers are always at one another's throats!"

The gentleman laughed.

"I can imagine that happening."

"You have no idea how seriously they take it," Farica said. "And it is the same with the farmers who vie with each other over their sheep and cattle. Those on the Earl's estate are furious if Papa wins a prize with his cattle or pigs."

Again the gentleman laughed.

Then he said in a different tone of voice,

"We are not talking about pigs and cattle but about you. Incidentally you have not told me your name."

"We should have introduced ourselves," Farica said solemnly. "I was christened 'Farica', and my father is Sir Robert Chalfont."

The gentleman held out his hand.

"My name is 'John'," he said, "'John Hamilton'."

Farica put her hand in his and as she did so she was conscious that his clasp was strong and firm and she felt something, which she knew were his vibrations, touching hers.

She was always very conscious of people's vibrations and she thought sometimes that she could see an aura around them that was either dazzling like a light, grey like a fog or at times black and frightening.

Now, strange though it seemed, she felt as if the gentleman in his cheap ill-fitting clothes was enveloped by a light that silhouetted him against the tree trunks behind him.

Then she told herself that it was just a trick of the sunshine and that she was being imaginative.

"Now we have met each other," the gentleman said, "I intend as the sage, whom you are consulting as regards your future, to give you my advice and hope you will follow it."

"I will certainly listen very attentively."

"What I am saying is very important," John Hamilton continued. "It is, because you are very beautiful and very imaginative, that you must never marry anybody unless your heart tells you that he is someone you can love and trust."

Farica's eyes were very wide as she said,

"That is what I thought myself. You have put into words exactly what I was thinking."

"So be very firm," John said, "and don't be inveigled into doing anything that you might afterwards regret."

Farica looked at The Castle and said,

"It is easy for you to say that, but it is very very difficult to oppose Papa and, of course, the Earl."

"Then play for time," John insisted firmly. "But whatever happens, don't allow yourself to be rushed into making a hasty decision or into hasty actions."

"I shall try – but it will be unpleasant."

Her voice was low and the worried expression was back in her strange eyes, which reminded him in their clearness and innocence of a forest stream.

Then in a different tone Farica exclaimed,

"Look what has happened! I said I was being selfish in thinking and talking about myself instead of you. You have inveigled me into telling you my troubles and I have not listened to yours."

"Very well, I will tell you mine," John replied. "Can you think of anywhere in the vicinity that is cheap where I can stay and like you consider my future?"

"I know of one place," Farica replied, "but you might not think it grand enough."

"I can assure you I am not in a position to be grand for all I possess at the moment is a few, a very few sovereigns, a horse waiting for me outside the wood, and the pistol that introduced us."

Farica gave a little laugh.

"It was certainly a strange introduction, but I am very glad I have met you and, as you have helped me, please let me help you."

"I am listening."

"In our village on the very border of this estate there is an inn known as *The Fox and Goose*. It is very small and is kept by a dear old man whom I have known for years. He is so kind and everyone who has an animal or a bird that is injured takes it to him, because he has healing in his fingers and he makes them well again."

"And you think that is where I should stay?" John asked.

"I am sure old Abe Barnes will have you, if I ask him to and I think too, if that scar on your forehead aches, he will take away the pain."

John smiled.

"If that is true, then I assure you Abe Barnes is the kind of man I am looking for."

"I will take you there," Farica said, "and the quickest way is through the wood."

"Does the Earl give you permission to trespass on his ground?" John enquired.

"His uncle allowed me to ride anywhere on the estate I wished," Farica replied, "and the gamekeepers and the foresters all know me, but I think perhaps you might get into trouble if you came here alone."

He did not ask the question but, as if he had, she said,

"The new Earl is not very kind to the local people. Because things had become a little lax in his uncle's time, he has threatened that anyone poaching a rabbit or caught in the woods will be taken before the Magistrates and perhaps transported."

There was a little note of horror in Farica's voice that John did not miss.

But he made no comment as she walked ahead of him down the twisting path through the trees to where she had left her horse.

Pegasus was free to wander and crop the grass.

Then as she whistled he came trotting to her side and John lifted her up onto the saddle and arranged her full skirt over the stirrup.

He patted Pegasus's neck and said,

"This is the finest horse I have seen for some time."

"He is my very own," Farica answered. "I love him and he loves me and, as you can see, he comes when I whistle to him."

"I am afraid my horse, which I bought when I arrived in Portsmouth, is not so accommodating," John said. "I have tied him to a fallen tree just around the corner from here. Will you please wait for me?"

He hurried away and watching him Farica thought that despite his ill-fitting clothes he moved with the grace of an athlete.

Equally it struck her for the first time that he was very thin and his complexion was sallow, as if he had been ill.

Then, remembering the deep scar on his forehead, she thought that, if it was at Waterloo that he had been wounded, he had perhaps gone back to Regimental life too soon and it had been too much for him.

A large force, after the decisive battle that had ended the War, had been kept in France to act as an Army of Occupation, much to the fury of the French.

She remembered reading that the Duke of Wellington had promised to reduce their numbers and now they were gradually coming back to England.

'How can I find him something to do?' she asked herself.

She knew that there were no vacancies on her father's estate.

In fact Sir Robert had taken on far more men than he really needed, simply because he felt sorry for those who had returned home expecting to be treated like heroes, only to find that they were an encumbrance and were looked upon all too often as vagabonds and ne'er-do-wells.

It was desperately unfair, but she suspected that many of them were in fact driven to rob, steal and even commit violent crimes because they were so desperate.

'I must try to help him,' Farica thought, as she saw him riding back towards her on a horse that was not, in any way as well-bred as hers.

But he rode it with an assurance that told her that he was indeed a good horseman.

They trotted along beside the wood, until Farica led the way into a ride that was wide enough for them to move side by side.

It was very quiet and beautiful, except for the birds fluttering in the trees at their approach, the rabbits scampering away ahead of them and the red squirrels chattering from the high branches in case they should steal their nuts.

"I had forgotten how beautiful England is," John commented in a low voice.

"This in my eyes is more beautiful than any other part of the country," Farica said, "and that is why – "

She stopped as if she was being indiscreet, but John could read her thoughts and he finished,

" – that is why you are considering accepting the Earl's proposal."

"Not really, but I would love to own not that Castle, which is very big and in which I might feel lost and frightened, but the woods, the lake, the cascade and the magic pool in the pine forest where I go when I am feeling worried and depressed."

"Perhaps if you have the time you will show them to me?" John suggested.

"Would you really be interested?"

"Very interested. And as you know, I am very worried and depressed."

"I can understand that, but I think you know in your heart that if you trust your Fate and perhaps yourself, everything will come right."

She spoke a little dreamily, as if she was looking into a crystal ball and John asked sharply,

"Why do you say that?"

"Because I am sure it is true."

"Just as I am sure that you must not and will not marry the Earl." John said.

She gave him a flashing smile. Then, as if she was suddenly shy, she touched her horse with her whip and hurried ahead of him and he had difficulty in keeping up with her.

They emerged on the other side of the wood that ran at the back of the Park and Farica rode onto a narrow country lane with the hedgerows covered in 'Old Man's Beard' and honeysuckle.

It was then, as if he was aware of it for the first time, that John realised that she was not wearing the conventional riding habit but a gown and she had no hat on her head.

As if she knew what he was thinking, she explained,

"I ran out of the house after Papa had been talking to me about the Earl and went straight to the stables to take Pegasus from his stall. As soon as he was saddled I came away to the woods so that I could think."

She gave him a shy little look as she asked,

"Are you shocked that I should be so – unconventional?"

"Not in the slightest," John replied. "I am only admiring you for being different from other women, who spend half their lives titivating themselves in front of a mirror."

Farica laughed and it was a very young and joyous sound.

"I never do anything that ridiculous, but Papa says I must go to London and be presented to the Queen and perhaps the Prince Regent and go to balls and Assemblies, which will need a great deal of dressing up!"

"But you would enjoy that?"

Farica considered the question for a moment before she answered,

"I suppose it would be an interesting experience, but I would so much rather stay in the country. I love being here with Papa."

John waited and after a moment, because she knew that he was expecting it, she added,

"It was only after the new Earl had come upsetting everything that I was frightened and worried – and you know the rest of the story."

"I have already told you what to do," John said firmly. "But it will be very – very difficult."

"Not half as difficult as your future will be if you make the wrong decision."

Just in front of them was the village green with the usual small duck pond, ancient wooden stocks and a pretty black and white inn with a thatched roof.

"Will you promise me something," Farica asked him, "and not be shocked at me for suggesting it? I know I am being very unconventional in doing so."

"What is it?" John enquired.

"Will you please – not go away without – seeing me again – or letting me know you are leaving?"

"Why do you ask that?"

"Because – "

She stopped and then after a moment a little hesitatingly she finished,

" – you have – helped me with my problem – and I may need your help again."

"If that is true, then I am very honoured," John said, "and I promise you, Farica, that for as long as you want me, I will be here."

Her face lit up like a child's.

"Thank you, *thank you*! Now I feel much happier than I did when I left home today."

When they reached the inn, John dismounted and lifted Farica down from the saddle.

She thanked him with a little smile and led the way in through the open door to find, as she expected, old Abe, not in the bar with its ships' timbers across the ceiling, but outside through another door that led into a yard.

There he was surrounded by his patients, some in cages, others in kennels and two in makeshift stalls.

He was sitting on a stool holding in his hand a thrush with a broken wing.

Farica stood beside him, but she did not speak, knowing that it might frighten the bird.

Only when his old fingers had in some magical way welded the wing together did he put the thrush into a cage at his feet and look up.

"I thought it were you, Miss Farica."

"I knew I would find you here, Abe," she replied. "I have brought you a very special patient who needs your help – in more ways than one."

Old Abe looked enquiringly at John standing behind her and Farica said,

"John Hamilton is a soldier who has just come back from the War, Abe, and as you see, he is wounded on his forehead. He is also bewildered at how everything has changed while he has been away fighting the French."

Abe smiled.

"Well, we'll see what we can do for you," he said. "Are you suggestin' 'e'll stay with me 'ere?"

"If you will have him."

"Any friend of yourn, Miss Farica, won't be turned away by me."

"Thank you, Abe, I knew I could rely on you," she said.

Abe looked at John, who held out his hand.

"I should be very grateful if you could accommodate me."

Abe studied him for a moment.

Then he said,

"'Aven't I seen you somewheres afore?"

John shook his head.

"I don't think so. I have been abroad for seven years."

"At war," Abe remarked. "And there's a great many as'll ne'er come 'ome."

As if she did not want him to make John feel gloomy, Farica showed him Abe's patients, finding a dog with a broken paw that she had not seen before.

"What happened to his paw and how did he get hurt so badly?" she asked.

"A trap, Miss Farica," Abe replied. "That's somethin' that were ne'er to be found in the woods in the old Earl's time."

"Do you mean," Farica asked indignantly, "that they have been putting traps in the woods at Lyde?"

"All over 'em, Miss Farica, and you be careful where you walks. They sez it be to catch vermin, but if you asks me, they're a-hopin' it's 'umans that'll suffer!"

"It is wrong! It's *wicked*!" Farica cried. "Why should the Earl wish to do anything so cruel when he has never cared for Lyde until now and never wanted to shoot in the woods?"

"I 'ears it's to be different," Abe said. "Smart gentlemen be a-comin' down from London in the autumn, just as there's bin wild parties with pretty ladies every week since 'is Lordship inherited."

The old man spoke in a condemning tone and Farica walked away from the dog with the broken paw and into the inn.

"I must now go home," she said to John who had followed her. "Abe will look after you and – "

She looked shy and he asked,

"Where can we meet tomorrow and at what time?"

"I don't know exactly what I will be doing," she replied, "but – unless I send a groom with a note for you here, I will meet you at the same place we met today, but you must be careful to keep to the paths."

Then she changed her mind.

"No! I think that would be a mistake! If you are found there without me – they might treat you as if you were a poacher and it would be difficult to explain why you were trespassing."

"Then where can we meet?"

"In one of Papa's woods. It is just up the road from here and if you go into the centre of it, you will see a clearing where the woodcutters have removed quite a number of trees, but it is still beautiful."

"I will find it," John said, "and I will be there at three o'clock, which will give you time to finish your luncheon and get away without comment."

"I hope so," Farica said. "I am sure you will be safe and happy with Abe."

"I am sure I will and thank you again for being so kind to me, Farica."

There was a deep note in his voice that made it hard to look at him and she moved quickly towards the door.

He lifted her onto Pegasus's back and seemed to take quite unnecessary trouble over the arrangement of her skirt.

Then, as she looked down at him, she realised that his eyes were as blue as the sea and she thought that even though his skin was pale from his illness he was nevertheless a very handsome man.

"Thank you once again, Farica."

He held out his hand as he spoke and she put hers into it.

He kissed it and she was very conscious of his vibrations, not only from his fingers but also his lips.

Then she rode away and, although she wanted to, she did not look back.

CHAPTER TWO

When Farica arrived home at The Priory, she saw that there was a caller at the house.

There was no mistaking the high-perched phaeton with the Earl of Lydbrooke's Crest on it and the same Crest embellishing the silver bridles of the horses.

Her heart sank since she would not now have a chance to be with her father alone and talk to him before she saw the Earl again.

She knew that the coachman with his cockaded high hat had recognised her and she thought that if she went to the stables and did not stop at the house it might cause comment.

She therefore dismounted at the bottom of the steps and immediately a groom came running to take Pegasus away.

She patted her horse's neck and said,

"He behaved very well today, Jim, and deserves a good meal as a reward."

"It be waitin' for 'im, miss," Jim grinned.

Farica went slowly up the steps, and when she reached the hall the butler informed her,

"The Earl of Lydbrooke's with the Master, Miss Farica."

Farica paused for a moment to tidy her hair in front of a gilt-framed mirror that she knew had been designed by Chippendale. Then she walked towards the drawing room where a footman opened the door for her.

She entered and was aware before they saw her that her father and the Earl were talking earnestly in a manner which made her sure that they were discussing her.

Then, as she moved towards them, the Earl jumped to his feet and her father said sharply,

"Where have you been, Farica? You did not tell me you were going riding."

"I am sorry, Papa, I did not mean to be so long, but it was such a lovely day."

When she reached the hearthrug and curtseyed to the Earl, he said,

"Better late than never. I was afraid I was going to miss seeing you."

"1 am here," Farica answered, but her voice was cold and she added accusingly,

"I am very distressed to learn that your Lordship has allowed traps to be set in your woods. It is something that has never been done before."

"I decided it was high time I stopped every Tom, Dick and Harry from thinking that he could poach my birds and snare my rabbits!" the Earl replied.

Farica looked at him and, although he was dressed extremely smartly and was in fact quite passably good-looking, she decided that she disliked him.

She had not been certain of her feelings before, but now she knew that she definitely distrusted the

Earl of Lydbrooke and nothing anyone could say would make her marry him.

"What sort of traps are you using?" Sir Robert asked of his visitor.

"Oh, the usual sort," the Earl replied airily. "They are meant for vermin, but if some thieving poacher gets caught in one it will ensure that he is properly punished, in fact probably transported!"

Farica gave a little cry.

"How can you think of anything so cruel and so horrible?" she asked. "The people of the village have always been allowed to go into your woods as they go into ours, so they will not be aware of your new restrictions until they are either injured or taken before the Magistrates."

The Earl smiled and it was not a pleasant look.

"What I have I hold," he said, "and I will not have people trespassing on my property."

"Your uncle did not feel like that!" Farica flashed.

"My uncle must have become senile in his old age," the Earl replied. "He not only tolerated vagabonds and poachers but allowed the farmers to fall behind with their rents and the cottagers to let their roofs fall into disrepair. It is about time someone pulled the place together and attempted to make it pay."

Farica stared at him incredulously.

"But you must be aware that things have never been so difficult as they are now," she retorted. "Now that the War is over, farmers are having difficulty in selling their produce, prices have dropped dramatically and even some of the country Banks are closing their doors."

She looked at her father as she finished speaking and said,

"You know that is true, Papa!"

"I am afraid it is," Sir Robert agreed. "Personally I am making every effort I can to help my farmers and I have reduced their rents for the second year running."

"You, of course, can afford to be philanthropic," the Earl remarked. "That is something that in my present circumstances I am unable to be."

He glanced involuntarily at Farica as he spoke and she knew he was thinking that if they were married he would have her large fortune to spend and there would then be no need for him to worry about money as he had to do at the moment.

Without intending to she had brought the conversation round to herself and she said quickly,

"It is such a lovely afternoon, Papa, why do we not go out into the garden? One of your azaleas that came from overseas is just coming into bloom."

Because her father was keenly interested in his garden, she knew that this would attract him and he rose to his feet saying,

"You are right. I could do with a little fresh air."

There was a moment's pause and Farica knew that the Earl was considering whether he should insist on joining them or should take his leave, which was obviously expected of him.

He decided to leave, but before he did so he said,

"By the way, Sir Robert, I came to ask if you and your daughter would dine with me tonight. I have an amusing party of friends down from London and I am sure you would enjoy yourselves."

"I am sure we would," Sir Robert agreed. "Thank you. Farica and I will be delighted to come to The Castle. Dinner will be at seven-thirty, I suppose?"

"No, I prefer London time," the Earl replied. "We dine at eight o'clock."

He put out his hand towards Farica saying,

"Goodbye until then, Miss Chalfont. Is there any need for me to tell you how eagerly I shall be looking forward to seeing you again?"

It was not only the way he spoke but his eyes, looking at her in a manner she resented, and the touch of his hand that also made Farica know that her instinct was right and he was repulsive.

Just as her vibrations had responded to the vibrations of John Hamilton, so she felt herself shrink away and turn back into herself when she was touched by the Earl.

Then to her relief he was walking towards the door and her father accompanied him to the hall to see him off in his phaeton.

Farica, however, did not move from the fireplace in the drawing room.

She looked around the room that been furnished in exquisite taste by her mother and recognised, although she could not explain it, that the Earl had left behind him an atmosphere of discord and unpleasantness which for the moment she could not avoid.

As her father came back into the room, she said to him quickly,

"Come into the garden. I want to talk to you, Papa."

"Of course, my dearest," her father replied. "At the same time I hope it is not something that will upset and distress me."

Farica did not answer. She only walked with her father beside her down the corridor that led to a door opening onto the garden at the back of the house.

Here were beautifully planned rose beds and beyond the yew hedge there was a Herb Garden that had been laid out in Elizabethan times when the house itself had been built.

The setting was lovely and Sir Robert had embellished the scene with exotic plants which had come from other parts of the world, besides planting not only roses but lilies and delphiniums, carnations and fuchsias, which made great clumps of colour that were exceedingly effective against the mellow rose-red bricks of the house itself.

Farica showed her father the azalea that he was particularly interested in as it had been brought to him by a friend from India.

Then he said,

"I was worried when you disappeared after luncheon, my dearest. I had no wish to upset you."

"I was upset, Papa," Farica replied, "and while I know that you do not wish me to speak of it, I have not changed my mind. In fact, now that I have seen him again, I am determined not to marry the Earl."

She spoke decisively, feeling as she did so as if John was encouraging her to be firm and determined.

Her father was silent for a moment.

And then he said,

"How can you be so foolish? And if you do refuse Lydbrooke, where are you likely to find a husband who can give you so much?"

"If you are talking about a title," Farica said in a low voice, "I want more from the man I marry than a coronet!"

"I know what you are going to say," her father interrupted. "You want to be in love. Of course every woman wants that, but love, my dearest child, usually comes after marriage."

"And if it does not? What can one do then?" Farica asked him.

Her father walked a few paces away from her and then back again as if he found it difficult to be still.

Then he said,

"I love you, my darling, you know that, but I am not going to pretend that ever since I bought this house and estate it has never crossed my mind that perhaps, if the Gods smiled on me, you would marry the owner of Lyde Castle."

There was silence again and Farica saw the pain in his eyes as he went on,

"Of course at that time I visualised that Rupert would be here in my place when I died. But now the house will be yours and what could be better than to use it either as a Dower House, if your husband dies before you, or as a home for your second son, seeing that your first will inherit The Castle?"

Farica gave a little cry.

"Stop, Papa, *stop*! You are planning too far ahead and I feel as if I am in a trap and it is impossible to escape from it."

"I have no wish to upset you," her father said again. "Equally Lydebrooke would give you the position I have always wanted you to have, one that you are entitled to as your mother's daughter."

Farica knew, because her mother came from an old Devonshire family, their antecedents going back into history before the Norman Conquest, that her father had always felt almost apologetic because his blood was not as good as hers.

And, as she had said to John, he was only a second Baronet. But why should she be concerned, she asked herself, with her father's ambitions?

Of course she could understand, of course she realised he wanted what he thought was best for her.

But it could never be best if it meant that she had to marry the Earl of Lydbrooke.

'Why do I dislike him so much?' she questioned herself and did not know the answer.

Because she felt that it would be a mistake to quarrel with her father and to antagonise him to the point where he might be more determined than ever that she should be the Countess of Lydbrooke, she slipped her arm through his and said,

"Let's talk about ourselves, Papa, or far more importantly, about the horses. I hear that there was a foal born this morning. Have you seen him yet?"

"No," Sir Robert answered. "Why did nobody tell me?"

"I expect they thought that I would want to tell you as a surprise," Farica answered. "Let's go and see him. I did not even peep at him until we could see him together."

Sir Robert was smiling as they left the garden to walk towards the stables.

*

As she dressed for dinner, Farica was worried.

She had no wish to go to The Castle that evening and she had the feeling that it was part of the plot that her father and the Earl were hatching together so that

~34~

she would be forced into agreeing to what they were suggesting.

Her maid, who had been with her ever since she had been a child, helped her into a very attractive gown of white gauze decorated round the hem, the sleeves and the décolletage with a pattern representing snowdrops.

The embroidery was so exquisite that they looked like real flowers and when she was dressed her father exclaimed as she came down the stairs,

"You are Persephone or the Spirit of Spring, my darling, and that is exactly how I like you to look."

"Thank you, Papa," Farica smiled.

She accepted her wrap, trimmed with swansdown, from one of the footmen and she thought, as they walked down the steps to where their closed carriage was waiting, that her father looked very distinguished in his evening clothes.

'And very very much nicer than the Earl of Lydbrooke,' she added to herself.

As they set off, knowing that it would not take them more than a quarter of an hour to reach The Castle, she said,

"By the way, Papa, have you by any chance a vacancy on the estate for a young man, a gentleman, who has returned from the War, but who would not, I think, be particular about what he does?"

"A soldier?" Sir Robert asked.

"In the Life Guards. He was wounded at Waterloo."

"How do you know of him?"

It was a question that Farica had anticipated and she replied,

"He is staying at the moment with Abe Barnes. I am sure that he will be quite comfortable at *The Fox and Goose*, but he has to earn a living."

"That applies to a great many men, my darling."

"I know, Papa, but we can only help them one at a time and as they come to us for assistance."

"Do you mean to say this man dared to ask you to assist him?" Sir Robert enquired.

"No, of course not," Farica replied. "But I do, in the circumstances, feel sorry for him. He has a bad wound on his forehead, although I am sure Abe will attend to that."

"Well, there is very little I can do," Sir Robert replied. "As you well know, we are overmanned already and actually I heard this morning that the Earl has dismissed three labourers from one of his own farms and turned the Prospers out of theirs."

Farica looked at her father in astonishment.

"The Prospers? But they have been at Biggin Farm for four generations!"

"Yes, I know," Sir Robert agreed, "but I understand that they could not pay their rent and Prosper has claimed that it is quite impossible to make ends meet."

"How can the Earl do anything so cruel and so utterly heartless?" Farica asked beneath her breath.

"I am afraid the answer is quite simple," Sir Robert replied. "He just cannot afford to live at The Castle in the way that his uncle was able to do before the War."

There was a little pause while Farica was adding in her mind the words,

'Unless he obtains a rich wife!'

As her father was obviously thinking the same thing, they drove on in silence until the horses turned in at the impressive gates, gold-tipped and wrought iron, with a lodge on either side of them and the heraldic Crest of the Brooke family carved in stone.

It led down a long avenue of oak trees where The Castle, now in the last glow of the sun with the first evening star beginning to shine overhead, looked lovelier and even more Fairytale-like than it had from the woods.

The thought, which she could not repress, flashed through Farica's mind that it could be hers. This was The Castle that had been in her dreams ever since she could remember and which she could never look at without feeling a little thrill because it was so ethereal and so beautiful.

Then she knew that however much she loved The Castle she could never in a million years love the present owner of it.

As they drew nearer, she found herself thinking of how all down the centuries it had been a focal point for the countryside.

Originally a Medieval Castle had stood on the site, but that had been demolished at the time of King Henry VIII, as had a subsequent building at the Restoration of Charles II.

It had been the present Earl's grandfather who, to the design of Robert Adam, had erected the present magnificent building. It had exceeded anything that had ever been built in this part of the country before and had caused even the King to be jealous of its magnificence.

'It used to be such a happy place,' Farica told herself as the horses drove over the ancient bridge that spanned the lake, 'but now – '

She did not finish the sentence in her mind, she only felt a little shiver go through her as she knew that the Earl was waiting to greet them.

When they were shown into the majestic, high-ceilinged Reception room with its three chandeliers each lit with a hundred candles, Farica felt once again that she had stepped into one of her dreams.

But it was certainly not 'Prince Charming' who came towards her eagerly with outstretched hands.

When she rose from her curtsey, she looked inadvertently up into his face and thought that the expression in his eyes was impertinent and seemed in a way that she could not quite understand a violation of herself.

Taking her by the arm, the Earl drew her to the group of guests who were standing at the far end of the room.

They had all, Farica discovered, come from London and she realised that she might have guessed it by their elegant appearance.

At the same time there was a decided immodesty about the ladies' décolletage and transparent skirts, while the gentlemen's cravats seemed excessively high and their fashionable coats fitted too tightly for comfort.

Then she saw that she was the only woman in the room who was not wearing glittering jewels, the majority of the Earl's guests having a bandeau or a tiara on their heads.

They paid little attention to her, except, she thought, to look disparagingly at the very small string of perfect pearls that she wore around her throat.

She knew that her mother would have thought them overdressed and over-bejewelled for a small party in the country.

When they went into the dining room, Farica was even more surprised.

As if determined to make his feelings very obvious where she was concerned, the Earl had placed her on his right, although she was sure that there were far more important women present and anyway the majority of them appeared to be married.

On his other side the Earl had a flashing-eyed dark-haired beauty who was wearing a profusion of rubies and a gown that was cut so low in the bodice and was so transparent over her body that she might, Farica reflected, just as well have been naked.

Then she told herself that it was only because she was so unsophisticated and had not yet had a Season in London that she was so surprised.

The whole party became noisier and more uproarious almost as soon as they sat down to dinner.

They had all been drinking champagne before Farica and her father arrived and it seemed to her that several of the men had already had too much, while the women's voices appeared to rise higher and higher every time they laughed.

The Earl, however, paid no attention to anyone but Farica.

"I have to see you alone," he said, as the first course was removed by what appeared to be an army of liveried servants.

"I am sure that would be – incorrect," Farica replied.

"Nonsense," he insisted. "It is impossible for you and me to talk with your father always present. I will take you for a drive and we can stop somewhere, perhaps in the woods, and leave the horses with a groom. I assure you I shall be very eloquent on the subject of how much you attract me."

Farica felt herself stiffening before she responded,

"I think what you are suggesting, my Lord, would not meet with my father's approval and you must be aware that it would be extremely unconventional for me to behave in such a manner."

"Come now," the Earl went on. "You and I need not stand on ceremony with each other. I want to marry you and your father has agreed, but we have to get to know each other."

"I think what you are saying, my Lord," Farica said, feeling embarrassed that this sort of conversation should be taking place at the dinner table, "is that my father has agreed to give his consent as long as I agree that I – wish to be your – wife."

For a moment the Earl looked disconcerted.

Then he said,

"Perhaps he said something like that. It's all a matter of words. When we are alone together, I will prove to you that they are quite unnecessary."

She knew what he meant by the expression in his eyes and looked away quickly.

She felt that if he touched her or tried to kiss her as he obviously intended, she would scream for help.

"The trouble with you," the Earl continued, as if he was following his train of thought, "is that you have been too long in the country and have no idea what fun you could have in London. That is where we will live when we are married and we will give parties at Brooke House in Berkeley Square that will go on long after dawn has broken."

He gave a little laugh as he added,

"In fact I can hardly remember a night when I have been to bed without the sun shining through the window at me!"

He laughed again and Farica looked round the table at the guests who seemed to be growing noisier with every minute.

She could imagine nothing more intolerable than parties where apparently the only thing the guests wished to do was to eat and drink excessively and laugh uproariously.

She remembered when her mother was alive the delightful dinner parties they gave at The Priory.

She had been able to tiptoe into the Minstrel Gallery before she went to bed and look down into the Baronial Dining Room where once the monks had eaten at a long refectory table.

Then she would see how lovely her mother looked at one end of the table and her father would be very impressive sitting in a high-backed chair at the other.

The table had been decorated with gold candelabra and gold ornaments with real flowers round them and the guests had seemed to be part of the elegance of the whole scene.

They had talked animatedly but quietly to each other and Farica knew that they would be discussing serious topics such as politics, national and local problems or perhaps sport.

When they laughed, it had been a happy spontaneous sound, not noisy and raucous, like the laughter that was echoing in her ears at the moment.

'Those are the sort of parties I want to give,' she told herself and noted with shocked surprise that one of the gentlemen at the table was putting his arms around a lady's shoulders.

Then opposite her a lady touched her lips with her forefinger before she pressed it against her partner's mouth.

"That will have to satisfy you for the moment!" she giggled provocatively.

As he caught her hand and kissed it, she merely laughed and made no effort to pull it away.

While Farica was shocked at such behaviour and disliked the way that the Earl paid her compliments, which all seemed to take it more or less for granted that she would become his wife, the dinner seemed to go on interminably.

Finally, to her relief, the lady on the Earl's left rose a little unsteadily to her feet saying as she did so,

"Now don't go guzzling the port until you're too 'foxed' to make sense. Join us in the drawing room in ten minutes or I'll come and fetch you!"

"To hear is to obey, my fair charmer," the Earl replied mockingly.

The lady then said sharply,

"And mind you don't forget."

Then she flounced towards the door.

Farica followed her, but the rest of the ladies seemed to draw themselves somewhat reluctantly from their partners at the table.

When they reached the drawing room, the lady with the rubies said,

"We have been told you are to marry the Earl! I suppose you know what you are taking on?"

"Nothing is decided – as yet," Farica replied shyly.

"Well, if you are as rich as he says you are," another lady said, "Fergus won't let you off the hook! You may be certain of that. He needs money, lots of it, and it's something he has wanted for a long time."

They all laughed as if at some private joke that Farica did not understand.

Then the lady with the rubies remarked,

"I hope when you are the Countess you will be kind to us. We shall miss Fergus if you take him away from us. Although he's always in trouble of some sort, he certainly keeps us amused!"

"That's true enough," another lady agreed. "I have told him before now that he goes too far. One day he will find himself in a mess."

"Not if he can buy himself out of it," someone else commented and they all laughed again.

Farica felt as if she could not bear to listen to them, aware that they were all assuming that she could not escape and that the Earl was marrying her for her money and for no other reason.

Quickly she said to the lady with the rubies who appeared to be playing the part of the hostess,

"Do you think I could possibly wash my hands? They feel rather sticky."

"Of course you can," the lady nodded. "Come along with me. I will take you up to my room."

They went into the hall and Farica then said,

"Please don't trouble to come upstairs. I have been here so often that I know the way. If you will tell me which room you are sleeping in, I can go there alone."

"You do that," the Lady replied. "I am in the King Charles II room, which I am not likely to forget, am I, seeing as it's the first time I have slept with a King!"

She laughed at her own joke and then walked back towards the drawing room as Farica started up the stairs.

It was then, as she glanced up at the ancestors of the Brooke family looking down from their gilt picture frames, that she wondered what they thought of what was happening.

She knew if the old Earl was still alive that he would be shocked and appalled at the behaviour of the guests at dinner.

She only hoped that it disgusted her father as much as it disgusted her.

She felt that it was an insult to the house she loved as well as an insult to the Brookes, who all down the centuries had fought and died for their country as the old Earl's son had done.

'It would have been very different, I am sure, if he had lived,' Farica mused and remembered how the old Earl had always spoken disparagingly of his nephew Fergus.

She walked along the passage and into the King Charles II room where she found an old maid tidying up.

When she saw Farica, she smiled.

'Oh, it's you, Miss Farica," she exclaimed. "It's a long time since we've seen you here!"

"It is, Annie," Farica agreed. "How have you been keeping?"

"Not too bad, miss, but things've changed since the old Master died. You'd hardly know the place now."

"What has happened?" Farica asked, knowing the answer.

"It's the people that stays here, miss! I've seen nothin' like them. The old Master'd turn over in his grave, that he would, if he saw the goin's on!"

As if she knew that Farica had come to wash her hands, she poured some warm water from a brass jug into the china basin and looked for a clean towel.

"You've no idea what the work's like, Miss Chalfont, since the old Earl passed on," Annie went on. "No one gets to bed afore five in the morning when we should be a-gettin' up. The young housemaids be so tired they falls asleep on their brooms! I've never known anythin' like it."

"I am sorry, Annie," Farica said.

"We're sorry for ourselves, and that's the truth!" Annie answered sharply. "But you knows as well as I do, miss, jobs be hard to find and there's quite enough bin sacked, as it is."

"Sacked? Why?" Farica asked.

"I think it's as his Lordship only wants people around him as be young," Annie said as if she was working it out for herself. "He's sent old Burrows away, who's been here, as you knows, for nigh on forty years!"

"I missed him when I arrived," Farica remarked, "but I had no idea that he had been dismissed."

"Well, he has, miss. So have all the gardeners who were getting' on for sixty, even though they were still capable of work, I can assure you of that."

"Of course," Farica said, "and it's their experience that is so valuable."

"You tell his Lordship that. He's not interested in anythin' except playin' games that make the house in such a state that it's impossible to keep it clean. And the destruction! You'd be shocked, miss, at the things as have bin broken since his late Lordship died."

Farica felt she could not bear to think about it and to change the subject she asked,

"Does his Lordship sleep in his uncle's room?"

"Oh, yes, miss. That is the Master bedroom, isn't it? And he says when he comes here, 'I am the Master now and you'll obey me or you're all out'."

Almost without meaning to Annie imitated the Earl's voice.

Then she carried on,

"And I'll show you somethin', miss, that'll shock you!"

Farica wanted to say that she did not wish to be shocked, but she did not like to hurt Annie's feelings.

She followed her from the King Charles II room a little way along the passage, where Annie opened the door of what was the sitting room connecting with the Master bedroom that the old Earl had used when he was too ill and decrepit to go downstairs.

As Annie opened the door, Farica could see by the light of the candles, and there were a great number of them lit, that the pictures that she remembered hanging there had all been taken from the walls.

She had not been in this room for a long time, but she could remember that one picture had been of the Earl's wife, one of his son and two others of his father and mother.

They had all been removed and in their places were what she thought were extremely vulgar paintings of women, some of them dancing.

One was emerging from the sea, while another was lying naked except for her hair on a rock in the sunshine.

They were crudely painted and yet they had an unpleasant fascination because in each case the woman's body was accentuated into something lewd and sensual.

After one quick glance Farica looked away and said,

"I agree with you, Annie, it does not seem right that the original pictures should have been removed. Where have they been put?"

"His Lordship told me to get rid of 'em, but I knew that was wrong, so I've put 'em in here."

As Annie spoke, she pressed a secret place in the panelling, which Farica knew the old Earl had always referred to as 'my special safe'.

It was actually a Priest's Hole constructed during the persecution of the Jesuits in Queen Elizabeth's reign, which had somehow survived the rebuilding of the house when it had been completely transformed at the end of the last century.

It now made a large square cupboard and, lifting up one of the candelabra from a table, Annie walked into it followed by Farica.

There, stacked against the walls, were all the pictures she remembered.

There was the late Countess, looking sweet, gentle and very lovely in her Peeress's robes and the old

Earl's father and mother, both having a dignity and a pride which she thought was apparent in all the portraits of their ancestors.

Standing by itself at the far wall of the cupboard was a picture that she only vaguely remembered and, as she had never met the Earl's only son, it had never particularly interested her.

"That's the Viscount. 'Master Ivan' we used to call him when he was a little boy and there wasn't a person on the place who didn't love him and look forward to servin' him when he took his father's place."

The emotion in Annie's voice was very moving.

Now Farica stared at the portrait, thinking that if that was how everybody had thought of him, it was very different from their feelings for his cousin.

Then something in his face reminded her of somebody and she supposed that it was the Earl, his father.

'Master Ivan', as Annie called him, could not have been more than twenty when his portrait was painted, which was, of course, before he went to the War.

He looked young and happy, his eyes were twinkling and his lips smiling as he stared out of the canvas with his dark hair was brushed back from his square forehead.

Then, as Farica looked again, she was suddenly still.

'It's impossible,' she said to herself and yet unmistakably there was something distinctive about his forehead that she had seen before.

In fact she had seen it only today with a deep scar on it and the rest of his face, if what she was thinking was true, was thin and lined from illness.

Yet still there was an unmistakable resemblance.

"Is that – really the Viscount?" she heard herself enquire in a strange voice.

"Course it is, miss! And a good likeness of him too. Of course, he'd be twenty-eight by this time and I expects that would make him look older."

"Y-yes – I am sure it would," Farica murmured.

"Things'd be ever so different if he were here now, very different," Annie remarked. "But there's nothin' we can do about it except pray God'll take care of him wherever he be."

The old maid turned away as she spoke to hide her tears, but Farica did not move.

She stood gazing at the portrait, feeling that she must be mistaken in what she was thinking and that it must be only a part of her imagination.

And yet the likeness was unmistakable.

Then she knew that she had stumbled inadvertently onto a secret that could be very dangerous to John.

CHAPTER THREE

As Farica came down the stairs feeling as if she had experienced a sudden shock and was not quite certain what to do about it, she saw her father waiting for her in the hall.

As she reached him with a question in her eyes, he said,

"I think, my dearest, that as it is getting late we should be on our way home. The Earl understands that I am getting too old for late nights."

It was the first time that Farica had ever heard her father say such a thing and she looked at him in surprise.

At the same time she felt delighted that she did not have to go back to the drawing room.

Even as she thought of it the door opened and a loud noise came from the room that echoed round the hall.

In contrast to the classical statues, marble pillars and fine portraits, it seemed inexpressibly vulgar and unpleasant.

It was the Earl who came from the drawing room and he said as he reached Sir Robert's side,

"I deeply regret that you must leave so early, but, of course, I understand. Quite frankly my house party, who arrived only this evening, are mostly just friends of friends and not at all the sort of people I expect to entertain after I am married."

As he spoke, although he sounded sincere, Farica knew that he was lying and she hugged her swansdown wrap closer to her, as if she would protect herself from him.

"Your carriage is outside, Sir Robert," the butler bowed respectfully.

Her father held out his hand to the Earl and Farica dropped a curtsey.

"Goodbye, Lydbrooke," Sir Robert said. "You know that we shall be delighted to see you when you have the time to visit us."

"My party is leaving on Monday morning," the Earl answered, "so perhaps I could persuade your daughter to honour me by driving round the estate in my phaeton. There is so much I am sure that she can tell me about my own property, since you both know it better than I do."

He spoke with disarming humility and Farica was certain that was all part of an act.

She heard, however, her father say,

"I feel sure that Farica will be delighted, but I suggest you come to luncheon first."

"I shall look forward to it," the Earl replied.

Farica walked down the red-carpeted steps and into the carriage that was waiting for them.

Her father joined her, the footmen closed the doors and they drove off, the Earl still standing at the top of the steps waving them goodbye.

For quite a long time she sat looking ahead of her, seeing not Fergus Brooke who had become the sixth Earl of Lydbrooke, but the face of the man who called himself 'John' and whom she had persuaded Abe Barnes to accommodate at *The Fox and Goose*.

Her father settled back beside her on the soft cushioned seat.

"I am sorry, my dearest," he began. "I am afraid that the behaviour was not what I would expect of a party at The Castle."

"I am glad you have taken me away, Papa."

"I saw the expression on your face when you left the dining room," Sir Robert replied. "But you must realise that most young men sow their wild oats at one time or another and I don't suppose that Fergus has been able to afford to do so until now."

"On the contrary," Farica asserted firmly, "I believe that the old Earl paid his debts over and over again."

"I cannot understand why you listen to servants' gossip," Sir Robert retorted sharply.

"It is not only what the servants say," Farica argued. "You must be aware that all our friends living around here talked about Fergus Brooke, even before he inherited, and naturally enough they are extremely interested in him."

There was a little pause before Sir Robert replied,

"What he obviously needs is the guiding hand of a good woman who is also sensible enough to make allowances for a man who unexpectedly comes into a distinguished title and one of the most magnificent houses in the whole country."

Farica wanted to parry that, according to Annie, he was treating his inheritance very badly in entertaining his dubious friends there.

But she knew that such a statement would only annoy her father and after a moment she said,

"I am sure, Papa, that the Earl should grow up and become more responsible before he even thinks of marrying."

Her father turned his face as if he would look at her, but by now the sun had long sunk, dusk had been succeeded by night and the stars were out overhead.

There was hardly enough light to penetrate inside the carriage and it was impossible for the occupants to see each other clearly.

"The Earl is impatient to settle down," Sir Robert said after a long pause, "and he feels it important that he should be married without a long engagement."

Farica thought to herself that the real reason was that he wanted the handling of her money and was finding it hard to live in the luxurious fashion he was doing now without the huge income the Earls of Lydbrooke had enjoyed before the War.

Every landowner in the country was suffering in the same way, their tenants could not pay their rents, farmers were going bankrupt and labourers were almost starving on the wages, which had been ample previously.

She also knew, because she was interested, that the last Earl had been glad that he had not owned very much property in London.

"It is the country that is important to the Brookes," he had said to her once when she was looking at the maps of the estate that hung in what was known as the 'Gun Room'.

"I have always been glad that Papa wished to live in the country," Farica answered.

The old Earl had reached out and put his hand on her shoulder.

"That is sensible of you, my dear," he said, "and when you marry, choose a man who rides a horse as if he was part of it, whose dogs obey him and whose cattle are well fed."

He had smiled before he went on,

"If he can look after them, he will look after the people under him and also his wife."

Farica had only been about fifteen at the time and she had laughed.

But somehow what the Earl had said lingered in her mind and she thought now that the new Earl and his friends would never be comfortable or at ease in the country.

They were part of the City and that was where they should stay.

They now drove on in silence until they had passed the cottages that stood directly outside the magnificent gates of the estate and were nearing the village green where *The Fox and Goose* stood and where the man who called himself 'John' was staying.

Impulsively Farica said to her father,

"When the Viscount was killed at Waterloo, Papa, why was his body not brought home to be buried in the family vault?"

She could not see his face in the darkness, but she had the impression that her father was surprised at the question.

"The answer to that is, I don't know," he replied. "It is usual for any casualty who was as important as the Viscount to be brought home with full Military honours, but in this case, as the Earl was so ill, perhaps it was overlooked and doubtless they found it more convenient to bury him in France."

They drove on for a little way before he added,

"I often thought that I should have brought Rupert back, but the Chaplain of his Regiment assured me that he was buried in a French churchyard with his fellow Officers and men and it seemed somehow wrong to disturb him."

Farica reached out to take her father's hand. She had heard the pain in his voice and she knew how much it hurt him to talk about the loss of his only son.

Later that night when she went to bed, she thought it very strange that if Viscount Brooke was dead, as everybody thought, he was not laid to rest with his ancestors in the village Church.

It held a Brooke who had fought at the Battle of Agincourt, others who had been killed in the campaigns of the Duke of Marlborough and some who had died in the Royalist cause in the Civil War.

If Ivan was dead, she reasoned, he would want to be with his own people.

She wished that she had asked the question earlier as to why he was the exception to other members of his family.

When she was finally undressed, she found it difficult to sleep.

She kept seeing the Earl sitting in his uncle's place at the head of the table in the tall carved chair that looked like a throne and was emblazoned with the family Coat of Arms.

Then she could see again, as clearly as if she was still looking at it, the twinkling eyes and smiling lips of the Viscount Brooke in the portrait hidden in the secret cupboard where Annie had put it.

'Why should the Earl have wanted to get rid of that particular portrait?' she asked herself and was sure she would not have to search for the answer.

*

Finally just before dawn she fell into a fitful slumber until she was awoken by the maids pulling back the curtains. She knew that it would be impossible to wait for the afternoon to see John and tell him what she had discovered.

All the time she was dressing she was feverishly trying to think of some excuse for sending a note to *The Fox and Goose*.

Then, almost as if Fate was on her side, there was a sudden thump on the window as a small bird crashed against it.

He was knocked unconscious for a moment and he would have fallen onto the sill if he had not caught his leg on a creeper and hung suspended swinging with the force of his fall.

With an exclamation Farica opened the window wide and caught the bird in her hands.

He was dazed but not dead and she thought that his leg had been strained from the way it had been caught by the creeper.

Only as she held it gently, thinking that it was very young and had perhaps fallen from a nest higher up on the house, did she realise that it was the answer to the problem that had been perplexing her.

"Is it hurt, miss?" one of the maids asked.

"I think it may be," Farica replied, "and if I put it on the ground it might not be able to fly and the dogs will catch it."

She paused before she added, as if she had just thought of it,

"I will tell you what I will do! I will take it to old Abe at *The Fox and Goose*. You know how wonderful he is with birds and animals that are injured."

"Yes, indeed, miss. When my grandmother's cat was 'urt in a fight he got it back on its feet quicker than she ever expected."

"Find me a little box to put the bird in," Farica said, "and make some air holes in the top so he can breathe. I will take it to the village as soon as I have had breakfast."

*

Not many minutes later Farica carried the little bird downstairs and put it in the hall before she went to breakfast with her father.

She told him what had happened and he agreed that it would be wise to take the bird to Abe.

"That man certainly has a magic way with everything in the animal world," he said. "I often think the village would not be the same without him. I hear that people come from all parts of the County to ask his help when their animals are ill."

"I think he is a dear little man," Farica sighed.

She ordered her pony cart to be brought to the front door. It was the one she used to drive in with her

Governess when she was a small child, but now she often drove it herself round the grounds.

She put the box containing the bird on the seat beside her and picking up the reins she set off, telling the groom that she had no need of his services as she was only going to the inn.

It took her less than ten minutes to get there and she jumped out eagerly, carrying the box to where she expected to find Abe in the yard at the back.

She was not mistaken. Abe was there and John was with him.

They were having difficulty in persuading a cygnet to keep still while Abe put a splint on its leg. Farica did not interrupt, but watched them until they had finished, although she was well aware that John kept glancing up at her.

Then, as the cygnet was put into a small cage to prevent it from walking on the leg until it was set, Abe said,

"And now, Miss Farica, I sees you've brought me another little visitor."

"It's a small bird that fell out of its nest and hurt its leg," Farica answered. "He banged his head against my window and then was caught in the creeper. I don't think his leg is broken, but perhaps you would take a look at him."

Abe took the box from her and setting it down on his knee lifted the lid.

Then she looked at John and said not out loud, but just mouthing the words,

"I must see you!"

He understood, nodded his head, and walking across the small yard opened a roughly carpeted stall.

"Come and look at the puppies that arrived during the night, Miss Farica. I am sure they will interest you."

Farica moved quickly to his side.

A Dalmatian bitch had given birth to six puppies and, as she looked down at them, she said barely above a whisper,

"I must talk to you immediately."

Then aloud, so that Abe could hear, she said,

"How sweet they are. I know they belong to Farmer Johnson and I must find out if I can buy one from him. Papa's Dalmatians are getting very old now."

"I will tell him what you want if he comes in later during the day," John replied.

"You're unexpected visitor isn't hurt bad," Abe said, "but I think, Miss Farica, he should stay with me for a few days till he's old enough to look after hisself."

"That is what I hoped you would say, but I feel it rather tiresome of me to add to your already large number of patients."

"They're never too many for me!"

Abe looked around the yard with a happy smile on his old face.

"Papa sends you his good wishes," Farica said, "and I was to tell you that he will call in to see you sometime, but at the moment he is very busy."

"Your father's a good man and a good landlord," Abe remarked. "Folks be happy on his estate."

He did not say anything more, but Farica knew what he was thinking and she asked quickly,

"May I take John away from you for a few minutes? I want him to move a branch that has fallen across the path where I drove into the wood. It might be dangerous if it was caught in the wheels of a passing vehicle."

"Now you take care of yourself, Miss Farica," Abe said. "John be strong enough to remove anything that's required."

"I am sure he is," Farica answered.

She went outside the inn and John helped her into the pony cart.

Then he asked a little doubtfully,

"Do you think I am too heavy?"

"I don't think so and we have not far to go."

He climbed into the cart somewhat gingerly and sat on the edge of the seat almost as if he was afraid that the cart would collapse under them.

Then, as Farica drove off, the old pony not exerting himself in any way, they did not speak until they passed the village green and were in the lane that led towards The Priory's gates.

Neither of them said anything until Farica drove off the lane and through an opening in the hedge that led her into the Park.

It was not a proper pathway across the grass, but was used by people on the estate who wished to reach the village and cut off a corner by not going through the main gates.

Farica drove until she stopped in the shade of some trees and then she put down the reins and said,

"Are you all right at *The Fox and Goose*?"

"That is not what you came to ask me," John replied.

As she spoke, her eyes had been searching his face, looking at the scar on his forehead and at his features that were unchanged, even though he looked very much older than his portrait.

As the pony put down his head to crop the grass, the only sound was the wind in the trees and the song of the birds.

Then Farica said slowly,

"I do not think that you have been completely – frank and honest – with me,"

"What do you mean by that?" John asked.

"Last night Papa and I dined at The Castle."

She saw his lips tighten for a moment, but he did not speak and she went on,

"It was a large, very noisy and in fact rowdy party and the Earl's friends who came down from London

~64~

were not the sort of people I expected to find staying at Lyde!"

"Nor, I am sure," John said, "were they the sort of people you should be associating with. Why did your father take you there?"

"The Earl invited us, and Papa, as you are aware, is very anxious for the Earl and me to get to know each other."

She did not look up at him, but she guessed that John's lips were set in a hard line as he said,

"I told you not to make up your mind in a hurry."

"I am not at the moment thinking of myself, but of my father's ambitions for me to marry the Earl of Lydbrooke."

John did not speak and, as Farica just sat looking at him, after a moment, almost as if she goaded him into it, he asked,

"What has that to do with me?"

"Quite a lot, I think," Farica replied, "because I may be wrong, but I think you are the only person who could tell my father that if he marries me to the man we were dining with last night, I would not be marrying the Earl of Lydbrooke!"

She saw John stiffen and stare at her in astonishment.

Then he said and his voice was harsh,

"What are you talking about? I don't understand what you are saying."

"I think you do," Farica responded softly. "Last night the old maid, Annie, who loved you very much and has never forgotten you, showed me your portrait which she had hidden away in a secret cupboard in your father's sitting room. Your cousin had told her to dispose of it."

John did not speak and Farica went on,

"That included the portraits of your mother and your grandparents."

"*Damn him*!" John said beneath his breath. "I suppose he is destroying anything that might be used as evidence against him."

"Then you *are* the Earl of Lydbrooke!"

"For what it is worth!" John replied bitterly. "But if other people are as perceptive as you, Farica, I shall not live long enough to boast about it."

Farica stared at him before she said,

"Why are you in hiding? Why do you not come back openly and tell everybody that you are alive and not dead as they all thought?"

He did not reply and she carried on,

"It is really quite simple. If you tell Papa who you are, I know he will arrange everything for you without there being too much unpleasantness."

"If you tell your father who I am, you will sign his death warrant!"

"What are you – saying?" Farica enquired. "I don't understand."

"Three men have already died on my account," John replied, "and I have no wish to add to their number."

Farica drew in her breath.

Then she bent forward, clasping her hands together, and begged,

"Explain to me! Tell me what has happened. I must know."

John looked around and then he said,

"As it is dangerous for you to be seen with me, I suggest that you leave the pony here and go into the wood."

He climbed out of the pony cart as he spoke and then helped Farica to do the same.

They walked through the trees until they found, almost as if it was arranged for them, several large tree trunks that had fallen down during the winter months and had not yet been collected.

Farica sat down on one of them and pulled off her bonnet.

She put it on the ground beside her and was aware as she did so that John was watching her.

"You are very lovely," he said in a low voice, "and very young. I have no right to involve you in this."

"But I *am* involved," Farica insisted, "and because I already know so much, I must know the rest."

"I can understand your feeling like that," John said, "but if I had any sense I would go away immediately so that you would not be associated with something that might so easily end in tragedy."

"I am not afraid and also I think it was not chance but perhaps Fate that made me find you yesterday in a place where I always go when I want to think. Having been brought so far, how can we be so feeble as to turn back?"

John smiled and it seemed for the moment to make him look younger and happier.

"Like all women," he said, "you can turn anything, however difficult, to your own advantage. Very well, Farica, I will tell you the truth, although every instinct tells me that it is wrong of me to do so."

"I have to know," Farica persisted.

"I am Ivan Brooke," John began, "and for what it is worth, I became on my father's death, the sixth Earl of Lydbrooke."

"Having admitted that to me, you only have to prove it." Farica said, as if she could not keep silent.

"I was wounded at Waterloo," John went on as if she had not spoken, "and from what I learnt later, I was knocked out of the saddle by a bullet that passed along my forehead, as you can see from the scar, and was dragged by my horse for some distance beyond the field of battle."

Farica was listening intently as he continued,

"That would account for my not being found immediately, as other casualties in my Regiment were. The scavengers that haunt every battlefield like ghouls stole my uniform and, of course, everything else I possessed while I was still unconscious and left for dead."

Farica gave a deep sigh, but she did not interrupt again and after a little pause John went on,

"When I first opened my eyes, I found myself in a Convent some distance from Waterloo, being nursed by nuns. They were very kind, gentle and understanding and it took me a little while to realise that I had lost my memory."

"You could not remember anything?"

"I could not remember who I was, in which Regiment I had been serving and whether I was an Officer or a Trooper."

"I can hardly believe it."

John gave her a smile before he explained,

"The wound on my forehead had gone deep. The doctors, and I can understand their diagnosis, thought that it was quite natural that after all I had suffered, and at times the pain was very bad, that it should affect my memory. Because I was English, they called me 'John'."

He paused and gave a little laugh.

"Actually I think they must have been clairvoyant because, as I expect you are aware, Ivan is only a variant of John, as are 'Ian' and 'Sean'."

"I did not know that," Farica said, "but I find it very interesting. Do go on."

"I should have been discharged from the Convent, but because they thought that I was not well enough to go out into the world, they kept me there when the other English patients had all been sent home. There were, in fact, only Frenchmen left who were very badly wounded and seemed likely never to recover."

He smiled again before he added,

"I think the nuns also found me useful because I am big and strong and could carry things for them, move patients who could not walk and help in a number of other small ways."

"Then what happened?" Farica asked.

"The doctors were still insistent that I must take things quietly and rest and give my memory a chance to return. Then suddenly I began to remember things."

"What did you remember first?"

"The lake. I could not remember where it was, but I could see it very clearly with the swans moving under the bridge near the place on the bank where I used to fish for trout."

"What came next?"

"The next thing, not surprisingly, were the stables and especially the stall where my stallion was kept and when I could remember his name it was a 'red letter day' for the whole of the Convent."

Farica laughed.

"What was his name?"

"'Twister'." John replied and they both laughed together.

"It took a long time," he continued, "because I kept seeing in my mind little bits of places where I had been and which I supposed meant something special to me."

"You did not see people?"

"Not at first, until one day in my mind I saw the portrait of my mother and knew who she was."

"The portrait I saw last night hidden away in the secret cupboard!"

"That is the one," John agreed. "There are other portraits of her in The Castle, but that was always my favourite."

"And did you know then who you were?"

"It took me four more days to remember that I was a Viscount, my name was Ivan Brooke and I had been serving in the Life Guards."

"That must have been very exciting!"

"It proved to be too exciting," John replied. "My temperature soared, I was put to bed and made to keep very quiet. I suppose in a way I had a sort of brainstorm. Anyway I don't remember much of the next week or so."

"And when you were better?"

"When I was better I talked to the Priest in charge of the Convent, an old man and a very kind and sympathetic one. I asked him to write to my father telling him that I was alive and to explain to him why I had been unable to get in touch with him before."

"You did not think of going home yourself?" Farica asked,

"Of course I thought of it," John replied, "but they would not let me. The doctor said that I was not well enough to face the rigours of the journey and, because I was still having blinding headaches that left me weak and listless, I listened to him."

"I am sure that was wise."

"Actually I think perhaps not. The Priest wrote the letter to my father and addressed it to the Earl of Lydebrooke."

"When did this happen?" Farica asked and felt that it was something she might have asked before.

"At the end of January," John replied.

Farica gave a little cry.

"By that time your father was dead. He was buried a few days before Christmas. I remember thinking how sad it was for the family that what should have been a happy festival was instead one of mourning and tears."

"Yes, he died before he could receive the Priest's letter," John said slowly.

"But as the letter was addressed to 'The Earl of Lydbrooke', I imagine it was your cousin Fergus who opened it," Farica said in a low voice.

"That, I presume, is exactly what happened," John agreed.

"And did he answer?"

John stiffened for a moment and then he said in a voice that was low with horror,

"He sent a man to kill me!"

Farica stared at him as if she could not have heard him aright.

Then she asked in a voice that trembled,

"D-did you say he – sent a man to – kill you?"

"It was only by a miracle that he did not succeed," John answered. "Because I was better and they had begun to think of me as a man rather than a patient, I had been moved outside the main Convent into an outbuilding where at that moment I was sleeping with two other men who had come in as patients."

John paused before he went on,

"I should explain that the Convent was regularly used as a kind of hospital in that part of France and in January, when I was waiting to hear from England, I was sharing what was no more than a wooden hut with a young farmer who had cut his leg extremely badly with a scythe and a boy of about fifteen who had broken his arm in climbing a tree. They were very nice people and I certainly improved my French in chattering away to them, because there was nothing else to do."

"Then what happened?" Farica asked.

"One night the farmer with the cut leg began to bleed profusely and I thought that somehow he had broken an artery. I dressed myself hastily and went into the Convent to find the nun who was on night duty."

He paused to explain,

"There was always one of them praying in the Chapel and, of course, I was forbidden to go near any of the cells where the sisters slept. It was a long way to the Chapel and when I got there the nun I expected to find praying in front of the altar was not there. She had in fact, I learnt later, been called to minister to a very old nun who had had a heart attack."

John looked without seeing in front of him, as if he was staring back into the past, before he went on,

"I stood about waiting, not certain whether I should return and try to cope with the flow of blood myself or try to find one of the more senior nuns who were more proficient in nursing."

"What did you do?"

"Just as I was becoming really anxious, the nun came back and, when I explained what had happened, she fetched the elderly Sister who had looked after me. It took a little more time while she dressed and collected bandages and what she thought she would need to attend to the patient.

"We set off down the cloisters through a door which led from the Convent to the hut outside. It was only as we were nearing it that I smelt smoke and said to the Sister walking beside me,

"'Can you smell smoke? There must be something on fire!'

"'There are no fires in this part of the Convent,' she replied.

"It was in fact very cold and I thought I must be imagining things. Then suddenly through one of the windows I saw unmistakably the light of flames and gave a cry of horror.

"We both ran to the hut, but it was too late. The roof, which was made of straw, had already collapsed and there was no chance of saving anybody inside. The nuns were all woken but actually there was nothing any of them could do."

"Why should you think that – the fire had been directed against you?" Farica asked.

"It was only later when they held an enquiry and the Priest questioned everybody as to what could have started the fire that it was learnt from the nun who was in charge of the Convent gate that a man, who she thought was English because he spoke French so badly, had asked if there was somebody in the Convent called 'Ivan Brooke'.

"'I want to see him,' the man had said.

"It was getting on for late in the evening and the nun replied,

"'I don't think it possible for you to see him at such a late hour.'

"'Where is he?' the man then asked.

"'He is not here,' the nun replied. 'This part of the Convent is only for women and men are not allowed in here.'

"He was so persistent that finally she told him that I slept in a thatched wooden hut at the other end of the Convent ground and that, if he called tomorrow, she would arrange for him to visit me.

"'It is too late now,' she said. 'Visitors must come at the time arranged, which is between two o'clock in the afternoon and four.'

"'And you think then I shall be able to see Mr. Ivan Brooke?' the man persisted.

"'I will arrange for you to visit him in the hut where he is sleeping,' the nun said, 'but come to me first.'

"He promised to do that, but, of course, the next day there was no sign of him."

"And you think he deliberately set fire to the place where he thought you were sleeping?" queried Farica.

"I did not suppose so at first," John answered. "It was only when there was no sign of my English visitor that I began to think it strange. Then two days later when he must have realised that he had killed the wrong man, the Englishman struck again."

"What did he do?"

"Because I could no longer sleep in the hut, which had been burnt to the ground, they took me back into the Convent. The whole episode in fact had brought on one of my headaches and a rise in temperature. The nuns insisted that I rested, but because I felt cooped up almost as if in a coffin in the small cell I had been allotted, I managed to persuade them to let me sit in the small garden in the centre of the Cloisters to enjoy the afternoon sun."

He paused for a moment to look at Farica before continuing,

"It was rather colder than it had been and frosty at night, but in the daytime just after luncheon there was some sunshine which was delightful provided one kept out of the sharp wind.

"They brought me a chair with a footrest and put it on the grass by a statue of the Virgin Mary that stood in the centre of the Cloisters.

"'You are not to read,' the nun ordered who was in charge of me, 'but close your eyes and if possible go to sleep. The air is good for you, but you are not, John, to do too much.'

"I promised her I would be obedient and settled myself down comfortably, thinking of home and how beautiful the trees looked in the Park when the frost touched them and made them glisten. I thought of how I used to skate on the lake when the ice was firm enough to bear my weight."

John paused again before resuming,

"I suppose it was thinking of all the things I used to do in the winter that suddenly made me feel cold. Anyway I knew that it would be a great mistake to catch a chill, which would undoubtedly make the scar on my head worse and I had risen to my feet, when a man who had been brought in the day before with a septic hand from a dog bite came into the Cloisters.

"'Are you off? I was just thinking how comfortable you look,' he said.

"'I am only going to fetch a coat,' I said, 'and perhaps a blanket to put around me. I feel chilly.'

"'I will keep your seat warm until you come back,' he said with a laugh.

"He sat down in my chair, put his feet up and his head back on the pillow that I had been resting on.

"'This is the life,' he sighed. 'I need a rest.'

"'Make the most of it until I return,' I said. 'I will not be long.'

"It was in fact quite a long way to my cell and when I got there I saw that there was a newspaper on the bed, which the nuns often gave me as a treat because they knew that now I was better I was extremely interested in the world outside and what was happening in the negotiations between Wellington and the French."

"I can understand that," Farica muttered.

"I read quite a lot of what the newspapers had to say before I remembered to find my coat and a blanket to put over my knees. Then when I went back to the Cloisters, I found that my enemy had struck again!"

"What had happened?" Farica asked breathlessly.

"The man with the septic hand who had taken my place had been stabbed through the heart with a long, thin stiletto-like dagger! I thought at first he was asleep. Then when I moved the blanket which covered him saying as I did so, 'come on, wake up! It is my turn to rest.' I saw the crimson stain on the front of his shirt and shouted for help."

"You were sure – it was the same Englishman?" Farica asked.

"A second enquiry, like the first, revealed the truth," John replied. "He had come to the Convent gate, explained to the nun that he had not been able to return to see me as he had hoped two nights earlier and appeared to be horrified when she told him that there had been a fire.

"'Is Mr. Brooke dead?' he asked.

"'No, he was lucky. He was not there when it happened,' the nun explained.

"'Then where is he now?' he asked.

"'I think he is resting in the Cloisters,' she replied. 'Shall I ask if you can see him?'

"'That would be very kind of you.'

"'You will understand that I have to get permission for you to enter the Convent to see Mr. Brooke?'

"'Of course and I am very grateful,' the man answered. "She left the gate telling him to wait outside until she returned and then hurried to the Mother Superior's room, which was some distance away."

"But when she came back, he had somehow got in!" Farica exclaimed.

"As she had trusted him," John explained, "she had not locked the gate, but only closed it."

"And when she returned?"

"The gate was still closed as she had left it, but there was no sign of the man outside."

"And the man – who should have been you – was dead in the Cloisters!"

"He was stabbed through the heart," John said, "and must have died instantly."

"This is the most terrible story I have ever heard!" Farica cried. "But what can you do? Surely there is somebody you can appeal to?"

"If I do so," John said quietly, "there is every likelihood of my being murdered immediately. Moreover I may be instrumental in condemning anyone who tries to help me to be murdered in the same way."

CHAPTER FOUR

Farica stood for a moment in silence and then she asked,

"What is the time?"

John brought a cheap fob watch from his waistcoat pocket, which she thought he must have bought in France, and showed it to her.

"Nearly half past ten. I told Papa I would take the bird to Abe and then meet him at the Church for the Service at eleven."

John smiled.

"I forgot it was Sunday."

"There will not be many people in Church," Farica told him, "as nowadays only the old villagers seem to attend."

Then she gave a little cry.

"But they are the people who will remember you, so you must be careful, very careful, that you are not seen!"

"I know that," John said. "As you must realise, I am trying to think what I can do, but it is very difficult."

"I want to talk to you about it," Farica said, "so I will meet you as arranged as soon as I can get away to the clearing in the woods."

"I know where it is," John replied. "I went there last night to make certain that I would not miss you."

Farica put on her bonnet, which she had taken off, and tied the ribbons under her chin before she said,

"Now that I know who you are I am going to pray very very hard that somehow you will be restored to your rightful place."

"If any prayers are answered, I am sure they will be yours."

She gave him a beguiling little smile and then hurried ahead of him back to the pony cart.

She knew that it would be wise to leave him to walk back to the house and hurried ahead down the field and out onto the lane, thinking as she did so of the terrible position he was in and already beginning to pray that God would show him the way without there being any further loss of life.

She did not underestimate for a moment the certainty that Fergus Brooke would fight like a tiger to prevent himself being dislodged from the position he had obviously always coveted.

It seemed incredible that any man should deliberately plot to murder his cousin, but she had heard so many stories about Fergus in the past, which she had not listened to, thinking that they must be exaggerated, and she was now prepared to believe that every one of them was true.

She had only to think of the party last night to shudder and she could hear Annie saying how many valuable articles of furniture had been destroyed by visitors when the new Earl invited them to The Castle.

'It must stop!' she thought.

But she was aware of how difficult it was going to be.

Farica had arranged that an extra groom should be waiting at the Church to take her pony cart back to The Priory, so that she could return with her father in the open carriage that he had arrived in.

He was sitting in the carved pew that traditionally belonged to the owners of The Priory when she walked up the aisle.

He smiled at Farica, thinking that his daughter was very beautiful and that she was exactly the right person to be the Countess of Lydbrooke.

Farica entered the pew and knelt down beside him on one of the crimson velvet hassocks to pray.

She prayed fervently with all her heart for Ivan, as she knew that she must now think of him. She felt as if her mother was helping her, telling her that all would come right in the end.

When the Service was over and she and her father drove back towards The Priory, its red brick walls looking mellow and glorious in the sunshine, Sir Robert said,

"I was thinking, my dearest, that no Countess of Lydbrooke could ever have been as lovely as you! And I know that a great number of them down the centuries were noted beauties."

"You flatter me, Papa, but as you appreciate, I am in no hurry to get married. I am far too happy with you – and there is so much for us to do together."

"At the same time," Sir Robert said quietly, "I want you settled and in a position that would please your mother before I die."

He spoke solemnly, but Farica gave a little laugh,

"That gives me at least twenty or thirty years' grace. I have no wish, Papa, to be hurried up the aisle."

Her father frowned and she knew by the angle of his chin that he had every intention of opposing her.

She slipped her hand into his and said,

"Don't talk of unhappy things today, Papa, let's just enjoy ourselves."

"We will certainly try," Sir Robert agreed. "But you have not forgotten that I have to see my Manager this afternoon. I know it is inconvenient on a Sunday, but he has sent a message to say that it is extremely important that we should have a conference as soon as possible."

"What is wrong?" Farica asked.

"I have a feeling that it concerns our neighbour's estate," Sir Robert commented dryly, "but I will be able to tell you more when we have tea together."

Farica made her escape from The Priory just before three o'clock. She had already ordered Pegasus to be ready for her in the stables.

She jumped on his back just as she was, without changing, and rode off in the direction of the woods.

It did not surprise the stable boys or the old grooms.

They were used to her riding on every possible occasion. They only looked after her as she rode away, admiring the way she sat in the saddle and the angle she carried the reins at.

When they were in the fields, she galloped Pegasus, only slowing his pace when they had to pass along the narrow paths in the wood that led to the clearing.

As she expected Ivan was waiting for her.

He lifted her down from the saddle and she thought that he held her a little longer than was necessary before he put her down on the ground.

Then he said,

"You looked like a Goddess from Mount Olympus coming towards me from the trees. I am only surprised you do not fly rather than do anything so prosaic as to ride a horse!"

"He is a magical horse," Farica laughed. "Don't dare think of anything else!"

"Of course," Ivan agreed. "How could I have been so stupid as to think otherwise?"

They both laughed and instead of sitting on a tree trunk, although there were quite a number of them, Farica sat down on a patch of grass and Ivan lowered himself to sit beside her with his back to a tree.

"I have been thinking about you and what we can do," she said.

"There is no question of *we*," he responded sharply. "I will not have you risking your life. You must allow me, Farica, to fight my battle alone."

There was silence.

Then she said without looking at him,

"It is my battle too!"

There was nothing he could say to this and after a moment she went on,

"I was wondering if there is anybody at The Castle whom you can trust, a servant perhaps who knew you and would never betray you, but who would be able to give you information as to what your cousin is thinking and planning."

"A spy in the camp!" Ivan exclaimed almost beneath his breath.

"It could make things much easier."

Ivan was silent for a moment and then he answered,

"There is a man, if he has not left, who would, I know, be completely and absolutely loyal to me whatever the circumstances."

"Who is he?"

"He was my valet from the time I left the nursery and it broke his heart when he was not tall enough to join the Life Guards when I did."

"What is his name?"

"His name is Hagman, and he must be getting on for thirty-five by now."

"I will try to find him," Farica said.

"No," Ivan said positively.

"I promise you I will not do anything foolish and I do think it is essential that we should know more than we do now."

She paused before she went on,

"Your cousin must have taken somebody into his confidence, perhaps quite a number of people. The man who tried to kill you in France for one and I think it unlikely that he would have crossed the English Channel alone. Papa always says that thieves and crooks, highwaymen and robbers always work in twos or more to give themselves confidence."

"There is something in what you say," Ivan agreed. "At the same time, Farica, I am terrified for you and I will not have you risking even one hair of your lovely head on my behalf."

"I think if we consider it sensibly," Farica said in a small voice, "the one person your Cousin Fergus would not want to kill – is me."

"Yes, of course," Ivan admitted. "Equally if anything should happen to your father or to anybody else you are fond of, I would never forgive myself."

"And I would never forgive you if you leave me to be pressurised into marriage to a man who is an imposter, a fraud and a murderer!"

She spoke violently and Ivan reached out his hand to take hers.

"I swear to you one thing, which is that I will prevent him from marrying you, even if I have to kill him myself!"

"Thank you, Ivan, that is all I wanted to know. It terrifies me even to think of it."

They went on talking for just a little while before Farica said that she must go.

"Papa is expecting me for tea and it is very important he should not suspect that I am doing anything except riding, as I often do, through the Park and into the woods."

"You know I want to see you again," Ivan said, "but because I think it might be dangerous, you are not to come here unless you have something really urgent to tell me."

"And you?" Farica asked him.

"I will come here every afternoon at about this time and wait hoping that there will be something urgent."

"I am sure there will be," she said optimistically.

Then, as she looked up into his blue eyes, they were both very still.

She had the strange feeling that he was wanting to kiss her, but because she felt shy she turned quickly towards Pegasus and Ivan lifted her into the saddle.

"Take care of yourself. I am ashamed and humiliated that I should dare to involve anyone so perfect and so exquisite as you in the mud and filth of what is happening to me."

"You are not to put it like that," Farica said. "Think of it as a fight, or rather a crusade, of right against wrong and of good against evil that we have to win."

For a moment he seemed almost spellbound by what she said.

Then he turned his head and said harshly,

"If I was half the man you think me to be, I would go away now."

"No man whom I respect would abandon his own people," Farica replied. "You are not fighting just for yourself, you are fighting for the old servants who have been dismissed after years of loyal service and for the labourers on the estate, who have been sent away without a pension. I forgot to tell you, the Prospers are having to give up their farm."

Now Ivan stared at her.

"The Prospers? I don't believe it! They have been here for generations."

"I know, but your cousin will not help them and like many farmers at the moment they are almost bankrupt."

"God damn it!" Ivan exclaimed beneath his breath. "I will prove my case and set things to rights even if it kills me to do so."

Farica put out her hand.

"Be here tomorrow afternoon," she said, "and I will try to make sure that Hagman comes to you, but I will not be able to come myself."

"Why not?"

The question was sharp and she realised that Ivan knew the answer before she replied,

"Your cousin is lunching with us and I promised to go driving with him afterwards."

"You should not do such a thing," Ivan said angrily, "and I have a good mind to tell your father so."

"Don't be foolish," Farica told him. "We have to allay any suspicions that he may have already so that we have a chance of catching him off-guard."

She saw the pain in Ivan's eyes before he said,

"Forgive me, I am making a fool of myself, but I cannot bear to think of you, so perfect, so sweet and innocent coming into contact with a man like Fergus. He is evil, I know it, but I am at the moment powerless to protect you."

"The fact that you are here gives me a feeling of protection and also that we are fighting what to all intents and purposes is a Holy War, which I know, with God's help, we shall win."

The way she spoke was very moving and Ivan reached out to take her hand in his.

For a moment he gazed at her and then his lips were against her skin and she felt a little quiver go through her.

Then he stepped back and said,

"Go, Farica, while I can still let you. And for Heaven's sake take care of yourself."

She smiled at him and rode Pegasus back the way she had come through the twisting moss-covered paths in the wood and out into the Park on the other side.

Then, as she rode as quickly as Pegasus would carry her back to The Priory, she knew that she had been right in saying that they were fighting a Holy War and that Fergus was representative of everything that was evil and wicked and he *must* be defeated.

*

Farica made her plans carefully and very early the following morning, when she thought that the Earl's guests would still be lying in bed after a late night of drinking and dissipation, she rode up to a side door of The Castle.

As a servant looked at her in surprise, she said,

"I wish to speak to Annie. Please ask her to come here to see me as I do not wish to leave my horse."

The manservant hurried away and it was some time before Annie came scurrying down the passage, her frilled cap a little awry on her hair and her white apron newly starched and clean.

"Why, Miss Chalfont, what are you doin' here at this time of the mornin'?"

"I am not making a social call on his Lordship," Farica replied. "I just called to ask you if you have found a very small ring on the washstand in the room where I washed my hands the other night."

"No, miss," Annie replied. "I've found nothin' and the housemaids haven't reported to me if they've come across anythin' when they was cleanin'."

Then she added,

"The lady sleepin' in that room went back to London last night."

"Last night!" Farica exclaimed in surprise.

"There were a bit of an upset, miss," Annie said, lowering her voice, "with another lady in the party. I understands they was quarrellin' over his Lordship and the lady as was sleepin' in the King Charles II Room considered herself insulted!"

Farica listened in surprise and Annie went on,

"In the end I has to pack up her things at a moment's notice. And she and one of the gentlemen left in a closed carriage with four horses, which should've made the journey quicker."

"It is still a long way," Farica observed, "but I suppose there was a moon to make it easier."

"If you asks me," Annie said, lowering her voice until it was a whisper, "she won't go far. She'll be back some time today. With all his Lordship's given her, her can afford to take a few insults."

Farica thought of the rubies, and there had been a great many of them, and suspected that Annie was right. At the same time it was just what she had wanted to hear.

"If the lady has left, Annie," she said, "perhaps I could just slip up to the room and see if I can find the ring. It was one of my mother's and I don't want to lose it."

"Of course, miss, you come up with me," Annie smiled. "Nobody'll see you at this hour of the mornin'. They're all tucked up in their beds, sleepin' it off, so to speak."

Farica dismounted and the stable boy who had been hovering in the background hurried to hold Pegasus.

Then she followed Annie up the backstairs, walked along the main corridor at the end of it and hurried past a number of closed bedroom doors before they reached the King Charles II Room.

As they entered, Farica saw that it had not been tidied since the occupant had left and there was, she thought, a terrible mess everywhere.

But she was not interested in anything except getting Annie alone and she went to the washstand slipping off as she did so, the little gold ring from the small finger of her left hand which she had truthfully said had belonged to her mother.

"Oh, here it is," she exclaimed, "under the soap dish. It's so small that it's not surprising nobody noticed it."

"I'm right glad you've found it, miss," Annie remarked. "You should be more careful with your jewels. Things that are set down in this house often gets picked up!"

Farica knew what she was insinuating and, glancing across the room to see that the door was closed, she said,

"Is there still a servant called Hagman here, Annie, or has he left?"

"Oh, no, miss, Mr. Hagman's here and he's always sayin' how disgusted he is at the changes that've taken place since his Lordship died."

"I heard he used to valet the Viscount," Farica said quietly.

"Yes, that be true, miss, and he talks about Master Ivan all the time. He could hardly believe it when he heard as how he'd been killed at Waterloo."

"It must have been very sad for him."

Farica paused and then she said,

"I wonder, Annie, if it would be possible for me to have a word with Mr. Hagman? One of the Viscount's brother Officers told my father something that I think he would like to hear."

"I'm sure Mr. Hagman would be pleased to have any news that came out of the past, so to speak," Annie replied.

"Then how can I see him?"

Annie thought for a moment and then she replied,

"I'm sure if you wish to see him so early in the mornin', miss, I could ask him to come here. Then I'll take you down to the side door and you can take my word his Lordship won't know nothin' about it."

"Thank you, Annie. I knew I could trust you."

"If you'll take a chair, Miss Farica, I'll be as quick as I can," Annie promised.

She hurried out closing the door behind her and Farica sat down and looked at the mess the lady with the rubies had left and which she was sure was very different from the way a lady like her mother or the late Countess would leave any bedroom.

There was face powder spilt all over the dressing table and the flowers, a pin cushion, and a hairpin tray had all been pushed together to make room for a large mirror that had powder and lip salve on its smooth surface.

There were hairpins scattered on the floor and a comb with a number of teeth missing, as well as pieces of cotton wool stained with rouge and eye shadow. It all looked unpleasantly scruffy and sordid and after a moment Farica rose to stand at the window looking out at the lake below.

It made her think of how Ivan had said that it was the first thing he remembered with the swans moving over it and the place on the bank where he had fished for trout.

She could understand that such a memory had been so precious to him that it had returned to his mind before anything else.

She told herself that things must come right. He must be back here in The Castle, looking out over his own domain and taking care of the people who trusted him.

The door opened and she turned quickly to see a small, wiry little man with thinning hair and sharp inquisitive eyes coming towards her.

When he reached her side, he said,

"I be Hagman, miss. I understands you wished to see me."

"Yes, Hagman."

Farica was silent for a moment, wondering frantically if Ivan was right and she really could trust his life, for that was what it amounted to, to his valet who was now in his cousin's employment.

Then before she could speak Hagman said,

"If it's about Master Ivan, I'd give everythin' I possess to hear somethin' about him!"

Farica did not speak and he went on,

"It was the darkest day of my life when I heard he wouldn't be comin' back. I never thought of him somehow as dyin' so full of life he always was and laughin' at everythin'.

"'Come on, Hagman,' he used to say to me, 'what are you lookin' glum about? There is always somethin' better round the corner!'"

Hagman paused and as his voice broke he said,

"But there wasn't anythin' better for 'im, miss, and it's only got very much worse for us."

Farica was certain that no man could speak as Hagman had without being utterly and completely sincere and so she said in a very low voice,

"I have something to tell you. His Lordship is, in fact, alive!"

For a moment Hagman stared at her as if he thought that she was lying.

Then he said,

"What d'you mean? What are you a-sayin' to me?"

"His Lordship is alive and desperately needs your help! But for reasons that he will explain to you, it is an absolute secret and you must not breathe a word of it to anyone, however trustworthy you may think them."

Flagman's shrewd eyes searched Farica's face.

"You can trust me, miss! I'd rather cut out my tongue than say a word that'd harm his Lordship!"

Farica smiled.

"He told me I could trust you. That is why I want you to go this afternoon at three o'clock to the wood on my father's estate known as 'Hawks' Wood'. In the centre there is a clearing that has been made by the woodcutters."

"I knows it, miss," Hagman said eagerly.

"Don't let anybody know where you are going. Make certain they think you are off to the village or somewhere like that. Then find your way to Hawks' Wood without anyone seeing you."

"I'll do that, miss."

The words seemed to come from the very depths of Hagman's being and she had the feeling that for the moment he was finding it hard to breathe.

But she had to be sure he understood.

"His Lordship is in danger, Hagman, in very grave danger and that is why everything has to be so secret."

Hagman nodded his head.

"I understands that, miss, and the danger be only two doors away from here."

Hagman jerked his thumb in the direction of the Master Bedroom.

"He would do anything to stop his Lordship returning," Farica said.

"That be true, miss," Hagman agreed.

"Anything!"

Farica emphasised the last word and she knew that Hagman understood.

Then she said,

"His Lordship is trusting you and so am I, with his very life! Now I must go."

Hagman opened the door for her and she found Annie waiting outside in the corridor.

Without speaking they hurried back the way they had come and, when she went out through the side door, she found Pegasus waiting somewhat impatiently.

The stable boy helped her into the saddle and Farica said to Annie who was standing on the doorstep,

"Goodbye, Annie, and thank you so much for finding my ring for me. I would hate to have lost it."

She waved her hand as she rode away and Annie waved back.

Then she was hurrying across the fields as quickly as she could to The Priory.

Her father, who was never a very early riser, was in the breakfast room and, as Farica joined him, she knew he supposed that she had come straight downstairs and had no idea that she had already been out riding.

"Did you have a good night, Papa?" she asked, knowing he sometimes found it difficult to sleep.

"Not bad," her father answered. "As you know, my dearest, I am inclined to lie awake and worry about you."

"I am quite capable of worrying about myself," Farica smiled.

"You have not forgotten that the Earl is having luncheon with us?"

"No, of course not. You let me in for agreeing to go driving with him this afternoon when I would much rather go driving with you."

"We will do that tomorrow," her father promised. "I want to see if there is any way that we can open the old slate mine and give a few other men in the village employment."

Farica bent and kissed her father's cheek as she passed his chair.

"I love you, Papa. There is no one kinder and more considerate than you are, which is more than can be said of our neighbour."

"You will have to talk to him about it, Farica," Sir Robert replied, "and, of course, when you marry, it will be easy to insist that your money is spent the way you wish."

Farica wanted to say that her father must be very foolish if he believed that the Earl would spend her money on anything that did not please him personally.

But she thought that to say so would be a mistake and she merely remarked,

"You know all I want is to have a great number of people re-employed and to have those wicked traps taken out of the woods."

It was something that she was ready to say again when, after a slightly uncomfortable luncheon, the Earl helped her into his phaeton.

As it was new, Farica wondered how much it had cost and suspected that the bill for it had not been paid. Nor, she was sure, had he paid for the perfectly matched horses that were drawing it.

"At last we are alone together! I find it impossible to talk to you properly when there is always somebody listening," the Earl began as they drove off.

"I cannot imagine what you could wish to say that could not be heard by Papa," Farica replied.

"Well, first I want to tell you how beautiful you are, and how much you attract me."

Farica looked ahead thinking that this was what she might have expected, but it seemed somehow trite and unpleasant the way the Earl spoke.

"1 want to talk to you about the estate," she retorted.

"What the estate needs," the Earl replied, "is money. For with the best will in the world, I cannot repair the houses, employ more people or increase the pensions without the wherewithal to do it."

He spoke sharply and before she could stop herself Farica said,

"The party you gave the other night when I came to dinner must have cost quite a lot of money!"

The Earl laughed.

"Good God, Farica, you are not suggesting that I should give up the few pleasures that are left to me? Besides a great number of those people were very kind to me when I was poor and unimportant and, as I am certain you will understand, I now wish to repay their hospitality and even offer them a few baubles."

Farica thought of the lady with the rubies who had left last night, but bit back the words that came to her lips.

They were driving down a smooth grass path that only became impassable when it was very wet.

At the end of it, Farica knew, was the Home Farm which traditionally the Earls of Lydbrooke had farmed themselves and which provided them with milk, cream, butter, eggs, young lamb in the right season and the best beef in the County.

She was, however, surprised when they drew nearer to the farm to see that much of the roofing needed repairing and the windows instead of shining brightly in the sunshine required cleaning.

The Earl drove his team up to the front of the farm, which was a very attractive Elizabethan building, half-timbered and with a gabled roof.

But to Farica's astonishment, instead of Bradshaw, a farmer she had known ever since she was a child, the man who came to the door was a dark, thin surly-looking individual who did not in any way resemble her idea of a typical farmer.

"Good afternoon, Riggs! I understand you have something to tell me."

"I have, my Lord, but you'd better come inside to hear it."

He spoke in an aggressive manner and in a half-educated voice, which surprised Farica and was very unlike the manner in which the farmers on this estate and their own had always spoken to her father.

"I am not getting down for you!" the Earl said aggressively. "I am taking Miss Chalfont for a drive and we cannot stop."

"I'm sorry you don't want to hear what I has to say," Riggs said rudely.

"Well, come round to this side of the phaeton and tell me," the Earl said, "and if you are asking for more money you cannot have it!"

An unpleasant smile curved the man's lips before he said,

"You'll be willin' to pay when you hears what I've got to tell you!"

"What is it?" the Earl asked impatiently.

Riggs walked round to the side of the phaeton and the Earl bent down so that the man could speak almost directly into his ear.

The horses were moving restlessly and it took him a moment to get them under control.

Having straightened himself, the Earl bent again and this time Riggs spoke.

Because she found it embarrassing, Farica actually tried not to listen, having no wish to intrude.

But because she had very acute hearing she could not help overhearing Riggs say,

"He be here somewhere."

There was a pause.

"Find him!" the Earl ordered.

CHAPTER FIVE

The Earl drove on and Farica realised that it was very important that he should not suspect that she had overheard what was said or that she was in any way concerned with his private affairs.

As they drove away, she therefore remarked,

"I thought that people called 'Bradshaw' worked on the Home Farm?"

"They did," the Earl replied briefly, "but I did not think them satisfactory and have given it to a man I can trust."

"It's such a pretty farm," Farica said in ordinary conversational tones and then continued, "but so is your whole estate."

"That is what I want you to think."

They drove a little way towards the woods while the Earl, concerned with his horses, at the same time cast many a sidelong glance at Farica, as if he was considering what he should say.

She was determined to be interested in the view and did not look at him directly until he said,

"You know what I am longing to say to you, Farica, and I think it is foolish that we should beat about the bush!"

Farica's eyes opened wide in surprise as she replied,

"I don't understand what you are saying."

"I think you do," he answered. "You know I want to marry you, and as quickly as possible, and I see no point in our waiting."

Farica looked ahead for a moment before she responded,

"Why should we be in such a hurry? I think it is essential that we should get to know each other well before we are actually married."

"I know you already," the Earl said, "and I know you are everything I desire in a wife."

Then, as she did not speak, he went on,

"I know, like all women, you are longing to make changes and improvements in the house where you will live and there is plenty of scope for it in The Castle and in my house in Berkeley Square. I am sure too you would like to make the estate a model of its kind and I am certainly prepared to leave that in your capable hands."

It flashed through Farica's mind that he was thinking that if she ran the estate he would be free to enjoy himself in London with his friends, like the lady with the rubies and the other noisy guests he had entertained at the weekend.

But she merely said quietly,

"It all sounds very fascinating. Equally, as Papa has told you, I have no wish to be rushed into marriage and I have not yet made my curtsey at Buckingham Palace."

"Good God! Is that really necessary?" the Earl asked.

"I know it is something my mother would have wanted," Farica replied firmly, "and I would like to do some of the things she wanted for me before I settle down and undertake the responsibilities that you have just suggested."

The Earl frowned as if he thought that he had made a mistake.

After they had driven on for some way in silence, he said coaxingly,

"Let's get married and as soon as possible, Farica. Then I will give you all the things in London you want, parties, balls, Court Ceremonies and a hundred others as well."

"You are very – kind," Farica murmured.

"Then you will marry me at once?"

"Oh, no, I did not mean that," she replied. "Please, I must have time to think – I must be quite certain that we would be happy before we are actually husband and wife."

The Earl's lips tightened in a hard line and she realised that he was becoming angry.

He was wise enough not to rage at her as she felt he wanted to do, but, as she had promised her father that she would be home for tea, he drove her back to The Priory.

After a footman helped her out of the phaeton, to her surprise she saw that the Earl was still sitting in the driver's seat, holding the reins.

"You are not coming in?" she asked.

"No," he replied, "I have something I need to do at The Castle."

He paused and then he said as if he was thinking it out,

"Please ask your father to excuse me from having tea with him and suggest instead that he lets me be his host for tomorrow after we have had another drive, which has been so enjoyable today."

Farica was about to refuse, but thought somehow that it would be a mistake.

It was important, she felt, that he should be kept busy driving her about rather than searching, as he might be doing, for Ivan.

"What time will you be calling for me?" she asked.

"Just after two o'clock and we will have a long drive before your father meets us at The Castle at four o'clock."

"Very well, I will tell Papa," Farica said, "and thank you very much, my Lord."

She dropped him a curtsey and then, as he drove off, she ran up the steps and through the front door.

It was such a relief to be home. But she had not forgotten what she had overheard at the Home Farm and knew that she had to warn Ivan.

She went to find her father, hoping that he would be busy and she would be able to make some excuse to ride into the village.

Unfortunately he was engrossed with his plans for the slate mine and wanted her approval of them.

They were all spread out on the desk in his study and he kept her talking about them until it was time to change for dinner.

It was then she realised that at some time this evening she would have to creep down to the inn in the village and warn Ivan of what she had overheard.

She was quite certain that since Riggs, whoever he might be, somehow knew that Ivan was somewhere in the neighbourhood, the first thing he would do would be to call at all the local inns.

It was after ten o'clock, when she had said 'goodnight' to her father and her maid had left her, before she was able to dress herself quickly and slip out by unbolting one of the side doors.

Because it was so late she did not dare to collect Pegasus as she would have liked to do.

She was certain that if she did the stable lads would think it so strange that she should be riding alone at such a late hour that they would undoubtedly mention it, if not to her father, then certainly to other members of the household.

There was therefore nothing she could do but walk the shortest way across the fields and through a small wood to reach the village.

It was not very far, perhaps three quarters of a mile, but because Farica was agitated at the idea of Ivan being in danger, it seemed to take her longer than usual.

It did not tire her to walk because she was always very active and actually as there was a moon in the sky everything was turned to silver.

It looked like Fairyland, she thought, as she hurried between the trees and kept in the shadow of the hedges until she finally joined the lane that passed through the village and went on further to the crossroads where the stagecoaches stopped on their way to London.

Everything was very quiet and most of the cottagers had already extinguished their lights.

When she reached the inn, there was a light in the barroom and she could hear voices.

She slipped quickly round to the back, afraid that Ivan might have been tempted to join Abe and his friends in the bar.

To her delight, as she entered the yard where Abe kept the animals at the rear, she saw Ivan sitting on a wooden seat nursing a black cat on his knee.

Just for a moment she stood in the shadows watching him.

Then, as if he was perceptively conscious of her, he looked up and she moved towards him.

"Farica!" he exclaimed in a whisper. "What are you doing here at this hour?"

"I had to come to see you."

He had risen as he spoke and now he took her by the arm and moved across the yard onto a piece of wasteland at the back where there were some makeshift stables where his horse was stalled.

There was also a miscellaneous collection of chicken coops, kennels and boxes that Abe used for his sick clients.

Ivan looked round as if to be certain that they could not be overheard and then he said,

"How could you come here and alone?"

"I had to," Farica answered. "It was too late for me to ride Pegasus – without somebody being curious about it."

"What has happened? Why do you want to see me?"

Farica told him what had happened when she was out driving with the Earl.

"Who is this 'Riggs'?" Ivan asked.

"I have no idea," Farica replied. "But the Bradshaws have been turned out and the way he spoke so rudely made me think that it might be he who tried to kill you and is now blackmailing Fergus into giving him not only money but also the Home Farm!"

"I would not be surprised," Ivan agreed.

"But you must understand what it means," Farica insisted. "You cannot stay here. They are certain to search all the inns in the neighbourhood and, although there are quite a number of them – they will turn up at *The Fox and Goose* sooner or later."

Ivan sighed.

"You are right. I had better ask Hagman where he thinks I will be safe."

"Is Hagman with you?"

"He came down to see me tonight," Ivan answered, "but he thought it wise to pretend that he was calling on Abe and to have a drink in the bar first."

"Who else is there?"

"Only two men from the village."

"But they might recognise you."

"Even if they have no idea who I am," Ivan said, "this Riggs will ask them if they have seen a stranger and they will point the finger at me."

"I will take you away from here to where you will be safe for the moment," Farica suggested.

"I told you I did not want you to be involved in any of this."

Farica smiled.

"I am mentally involved, you know that! We must get hold of Hagman and tell him where I am taking you."

"He should be out at any moment," Ivan said.

His eyes were on Farica's face in the moonlight and he spoke as if he was thinking of something else.

Then abruptly he turned away and walked back to the gate that let them into the yard.

Farica had the idea that he had been about to tell her something of importance and she wanted to hear it.

But, as she caught him up, she saw Hagman coming into the yard of the inn.

Ivan beckoned him to where they were standing and then he said,

"Has everybody left?"

"All except one man, my Lord," Hagman said, "and he's very old and almost blind."

"Nevertheless, Hagman, tell Abe to come out here. You can say that one of the animals appears to be in pain."

Without saying anything more Hagman walked back across the yard and opened the inn door and Farica heard him shout,

"Hi, Abe! One of your patients is complainin' he's not gettin' enough attention."

"I'm a'comin'. I'm a'comin'," Abe said and then Farica heard him say to somebody else,

"You let yoursel out, Bill."

"I can do that after nigh on sixty years!" the old man replied.

Then Abe came out of the inn and closed the door behind him.

As if he sensed that he had been called to Ivan rather than to one of his animals or birds, he walked straight across the yard towards him.

"What is it?" he asked. "Anythin' wrong?"

"It's only that I have to go away tonight," Ivan replied, 'and I wanted to thank you for your hospitality and tell you I shall be back very shortly."

"You're leavin' tonight?"

"At once," Ivan replied. "But I wanted to give you something that will help the animals, especially the young cygnet you have worked so hard on."

Abe chuckled.

Farica, who was standing back in the shadows where she could not be seen, saw Ivan put some money into Abe's hand.

The old man would have refused it, but Ivan insisted that it was for those who needed it, saying even splints, lotions and bandages did not grow on gooseberry bushes.

Abe chuckled again and then he said,

"Now, you take good care of yoursel and you're welcome to come back any time as suits you."

"Thank you very much," Ivan smiled.

He waited until Abe had gone back into the inn and then he said to Hagman,

"Fetch my things and join me at the clearing in the wood. I will wait for you there."

"Very well, my Lord," Hagman agreed in a whisper.

He followed Abe and Farica thought that he would tell the old man that Ivan had sent him to collect something for him and that they were travelling together.

Then all she could think of was that Ivan was beside her again and they moved quickly to the stable where his horse was waiting.

He started to saddle him and as he did so Farica said,

"I did not ask you what you call him."

Ivan was slipping the bridle over his horse's nose as he replied,

"Waterloo, of course! What else?"

They both laughed and he added,

"That is what I am facing at the moment, Farica, my Waterloo, and it will either be a great victory or an ignominious retreat!"

"You know the answer to that," Farica answered in a low voice.

They brought Waterloo out into the moonlight and when she was not expecting it, Ivan picked her up and placed her on the saddle.

She did not, however, protest as he swung himself up behind her and they set off, keeping out of sight of the houses until they reached the path that led towards The Priory.

"How did you know that I was taking you somewhere near my home?" Farica asked.

"I can read your thoughts," Ivan answered, "and besides I cannot believe that my own land would be very healthy for me at this particular moment."

There was an inflection in his voice that made her look up at him as if she wanted to comfort him.

As she did so, she was suddenly aware of how close she was against him, that his arm was around her and their faces were only a few inches apart.

She had ridden in front of a man's saddle since she had been a small child and her father had carried her that way on one of his great stallions.

Now she was aware of how intimate it was and how it was impossible for her body not to touch Ivan's.

They were riding without speaking, but then she felt in some strange manner that they were saying a thousand things to each other and had no need for words.

Just as she had done on her way to the village, Ivan kept in the shadows first of the hedges and then of the trees until they reached the wood.

He made no attempt to hasten and she knew that it was because he thought to do so would make it uncomfortable for her.

And yet because he was holding her close against him she thought that she had never felt so safe or so happy in her whole life.

Ivan was in danger and she might be as well, but they were together, his arm was around her and she thought that her heart was doing strange things in her breast.

Now they were in the wood and there was a silence created by the trees and the faint sounds that came from small animals hurrying away through the undergrowth at their approach.

Then there would be the sudden flight of a bird coming off the roost because they had passed immediately underneath him.

They reached the clearing where the moonlight seemed dazzling in its brightness and instinctively Farica turned her head to look up at Ivan because she was sure that he found it as magical as she did.

It was then that he dropped the reins, put his other arm around her and his lips found hers.

For one instant it was a surprise to Farica. Then she knew that, almost without knowing it, it was what she had longed for and prayed for ever since she had met him.

He kissed her fiercely and demandingly as if he could not control himself.

Then, as he felt the softness of her mouth and the little quiver that went through her, he became more gentle, tender and yet possessive, as if he wooed her with his kisses.

He kissed her until Farica felt as if the moonlight had entered into both of them and joined them with a radiance that could only have come from Heaven itself.

She had never been kissed and the sensations that Ivan gave her were so wonderful and so different from anything she had ever known or even imagined in her wildest dreams that she felt as if they both moved on shafts of light up to the moon itself.

They were no longer human, no longer on Earth, but part of the Heavenly Sphere and the stars were not only all around them but in their hearts and minds, their eyes and lips.

Only as Farica felt as if she had touched Heaven and would never come back to Earth did Ivan raise his head and say,

"God, how I love you! My darling, I did not mean to do this tonight or at any time until I am a free man."

"I – love you!"

Because her voice had a rapture and ecstasy in it that told him what she was feeling, Ivan kissed her again.

She could feel his heart beating against hers and he knew that never in his life had he known such ecstasy.

Then, as if he was suddenly aware that they were still sitting on the back of Waterloo, who was cropping the rather sparse grass in the clearing, Ivan swung himself down on the ground and then lifted Farica from the saddle.

He did not, however, put her down, but holding her cradled in his arms he kissed her until without really meaning to she put up her hands in protest.

Instantly she was free, except that he kept one arm around her as if to steady her.

"Forgive me," he said, "but you go to my head and I cannot think sanely about anything when I am so near you."

It was then that the reason for her coming to him in the first place was back in her mind.

And yet it was hard to think of anything except that his kisses made her feel as if she had come alive and her whole body was pulsating with the wonder of him.

"I – love you!" she murmured again.

"And I love you!"

Three simple words, but she knew that they came from the very depths of his heart and were spoken with a sincerity that could not have been more sacred if he had said them to her in a Cathedral.

Then, as they gazed at each other, their eyes, reflecting not only the moonlight but also the radiant light of love that came from within them, they heard Hagman coming through the wood.

He joined them a few moments later carrying a bundle, which Farica guessed was all that Ivan possessed, except what he stood up in.

"It was lucky that you were there tonight," she said to Hagman, "otherwise I was wondering how I could get word to you as to where I was hiding your Master."

"Where do we go from here?" Ivan asked.

"I will have to show you or you will never find it and it will be easier to walk than to ride."

"I will walk," he said, "and, as I shall be leading Waterloo, you can ride."

Again he lifted her into the saddle and gave her the reins.

Then he walked as Farica directed along a twisting path between a number of fir trees that brought them out on the outside of the garden of The Priory.

They had been moving in silence until Farica now said,

"The path ahead is likely to be overgrown as no one has used it for a long time."

She slipped down from the saddle onto the ground and walked ahead to show them the way, Ivan following her with Waterloo and Hagman behind.

The path twisted between the trees until suddenly in the very centre of a large clump of rhododendrons there was a small house.

It was so tiny that it was little more than a shed, but, as the moonlight illuminated it, Ivan could see that it looked rather like a house out of a Fairytale with a high thatched roof and blue shutters covering the windows.

Farica opened the door with a key she had brought with her in her pocket and, although she could just about stand up to go inside, Ivan had to bow his head to follow her.

It took them a few minutes to find the tinderbox and to light the candle lantern that hung from the rafters in the centre of the room.

When it was lit, in order to make it easier to see, Farica opened the shutters that covered the windows.

Ivan stared around in amazement and Farica laughed.

"Papa built this for me when I was ten," she explained. "It was my own special doll's house, but large enough for me."

"I have never seen anything so amazing," Ivan exclaimed.

"I adored it," Farica smiled, "and, although you may feel rather like a giant in it, it is very unlikely that anyone will think of looking for you here. At least it is a roof over your head, and the bed will be just big enough for you."

The house was divided into two portions, first a sitting room that was beautifully furnished with a carpet on the floor, a fireplace, chairs that were small, but just big enough for a grown-up to sit in and the same applied to the sofa.

There was a table to eat at with pretty chairs with velvet-covered seats and the pictures on the walls were all of fairies and goblins.

In the bedroom there was the bed that Farica had used and several doll's beds as well as a small dressing table and washstand that were just the right size for a little girl of ten.

Ivan looked round and said,

"Only you could produce something so fantastic! When I first saw you, I thought that you had stepped out of Fairyland and now I know I was right!"

"And this is the – Fairy House in the wood," Farica replied, "which I am quite certain will be invisible to anyone – who is looking for you."

She tried to speak confidently, but there was a tremor in her voice, as if she was afraid, and Ivan took a step towards her as if he would take her in his arms.

Then he remembered that Hagman was outside.

"There is also a special place for Waterloo," Farica continued, "because I often used to come here on my pony and Papa made a little stable for him where I could groom him myself."

They went outside and she showed Ivan where Waterloo could be stabled.

It was rather small, but there was a manger and a bucket that he could drink from and straw on the ground.

They took Waterloo's bridle and saddle from him and he went into the stall and seemed perfectly content.

"What do you think of it, Hagman?" Ivan asked.

"If I wasn't a seein' it with me own two eyes, my Lord," Hagman replied, "I'd say I'd had one too many at *The Fox and Goose*!"

Ivan laughed and then he declared,

"Now you know where to find me and I shall keep out of sight here until you can tell me – what is being planned for me."

"I'll keep me eyes and ears open, my Lord, don't you worry about that and I'll be over to see you as soon as I can get away."

"Thank you very much, Hagman," and if you can, bring me a newspaper. I want to be sure there is still a world outside this one."

"Leave it to me, my Lord. Goodnight."

He looked at Farica and said,

"And goodnight to you, miss. This be a surprise and make no mistake, but his Lordship'll be safer here than anywhere else."

"I am sure he will be," Farica answered.

Hagman went off through the trees and they knew that it was not a long distance across country from here to The Castle.

Farica closed the shutters that were letting in the moonlight because she was afraid that the light from the lantern might in some way be seen through the trees.

Then, as if Ivan thought that it was a mistake for her to be alone with him inside the house, he went out through the front door to stand on the little terrace that had been erected by her father.

The rhododendrons had grown since they had been planted until the house was almost lost amongst them.

"I am sure you will – be safe here," Farica said as if she was reassuring herself.

"Nothing could be more enchanting, except you!"

Farica smiled up at him and then said,

"Tomorrow morning early, very early, so that no one will see me, I will bring you some food. Oh and I forgot to show you a tiny well outside by the stable. The water is absolutely pure as it comes straight down from the hill at the top of the woods."

"What more could anyone want?" Ivan asked.

He was joking, but it flashed through her mind and she knew it flashed through his, that he did not wish to live in a doll's house but in The Castle that was his own and which had been his father's and his ancestors' before him.

"I had better go back," Farica said reluctantly.

"You know I don't want you to go," Ivan replied,

"But I am terrified of hurting you in any way and even gossip can be dangerous."

"I am not afraid of that."

"You are so perfect," Ivan said, "that I would not have anyone say a word against you. All I wish to do myself is to kneel before you as if you are a Saint and thank you for all you have done for me."

He put his arm around her as he spoke and, tipping her face up to his, he looked at her for a long moment.

"No one could ever be lovelier," he said, "and I can only say that I will fight for you and defend and protect you for the rest of my life."

The way he spoke was very moving and Farica felt herself quiver because he was touching her and because she loved him.

"We are going to win," she said, "there is no doubt of it. But please be very careful of yourself because you know that the forces of evil are ranged against you."

She saw the expression in Ivan's eyes and knew how much he resented the fact that he was to all intents and purposes powerless and he loathed having to hide and scheme rather than attack his enemy in the open.

She knew exactly what he was thinking and because she wanted to comfort as well as inspire him she put her arms around him and drew his head down to hers.

"I love you," she said, "and our love – must be invincible."

He held her so tightly that it was impossible to breathe.

Then once again he was kissing her wildly and passionately as if the fires within him were ignited and flaring violently like a forest fire.

He kissed her lips, her eyes, the softness of her neck, giving her strange sensations that she had never known before and yet she was not afraid.

She realised that he must express what had been kept hidden for so long and now burst from him like a volcano that suddenly erupts.

He kissed her until the moonlight seemed to swing dizzily around them and they were no longer standing amongst the rhododendrons and in the shadow of the trees, but were sailing on shafts of light up into the sky.

"I love you – *I love you*!" Farica wanted to shout out, but it was impossible to speak.

She could only feel her heart beating and a fire burning within her that came from the fire on Ivan's lips.

Only when they were both breathless did he say,

"Forgive me, I should have sent you home ages ago, but, my darling, I would not frighten you."

"I am not afraid," Farica said, "but I did not understand that love was so exciting and so completely different from what I expected."

He laughed gently and asked,

"What did you expect?"

"I always thought that love would be very quiet, soft and sweet, rather like music from a violin or perhaps the song of the birds."

"And now?"

"It is overwhelming – stupendous! Like being swept along on a chariot of fire so glorious that I feel as if I am enchanted."

"I think that is what you are." Ivan said, "and because you love me, I am enchanted too. We are no longer human, my precious, but have become as Gods and as Gods we are unconquerable."

He held her close against him as he went on,

"You have inspired me and made me aware that I am more of a man than I have ever been before."

"I love you – as a man."

"I love you as a woman, *my* woman, and no one shall ever take you from me."

He looked down at her for a moment before he said,

"Supposing, just supposing I am unable to reclaim my rightful place as my father's son? Suppose I fail and yet remain alive? Will you still marry me?"

Farica laughed and it was a very happy sound.

"Do you really believe for a moment that I love you – because you are an Earl?" she asked. "I love you because, as I have said, you are a man. I love you because from the very first moment I met you, I knew that you were something special and different from anybody I have known before."

Her voice softened as she continued,

"When you turned to look at me – I felt that there was a light coming from you that silhouetted you against the tree trunks. Then I told myself it was the sunshine."

"And to me you have been illuminated by a light ever since I saw you standing a little way from me and thought that you were a nymph of the trees," Ivan said, "and so different and so inescapable that you stole my heart and it has never been mine since."

"That is what I wanted to know, Ivan. Whatever happens, will you swear we will never lose each other?"

"I swear it!" Ivan asserted firmly. "And if it is impossible for us to live at The Castle, then I will build a Castle for you somewhere else, even if I do it with my own hands. What really matters, Farica, is that you are, mine, mine completely and I cannot lose you."

He kissed her again and this time she felt as if there was something desperate about it, as if he was afraid not only for himself and the position that had been stolen from him but of losing her.

"Because tonight we are both enchanted," she murmured softly, "I know, as an enchantress, that everything will come right. We may have to labour like Hercules to achieve what is right and just, but we will be successful as long as we do it together."

Ivan kissed her hand and then he said,

"You are perfect, but now go to bed, my darling, while I can let you. One day, God willing, we will be married, then not even the night shall separate us. But now I have to let you go."

Farica kissed him gently on the cheek and instantly the fire swept away the solemnity of his eyes and his lips were seeking hers.

He kissed her until she felt that he drew her very heart from her body and made it his.

"I want you, oh God, I want you," he breathed.

Then abruptly, as if flesh and blood could stand no more, he walked away from her into the little doll's house and closed the door behind him.

For a moment she could hardly believe that he had gone.

Her heart was beating so tumultuously and she felt as if the world was swimming around her.

Then, because she knew it was right, she ran away through the bushes towards The Priory.

As she went, her heart was singing and she was saying over and over again,

'Thank You, God, *thank You*. He loves me, as I love him, and nothing else is really of any consequence!'

CHAPTER SIX

Farica rose very early in the morning, well before five o'clock when she knew that the maids would be coming downstairs to open up the house.

As she crept along the shrouded corridors, she thought that if her father knew what was happening he would be horrified, and so, if she was alive, would her mother.

And yet she was aware that there was nothing she could do at the moment but try to help Ivan in every way she could.

She knew that he was not exaggerating when he said that Fergus was very dangerous and, although it seemed incredible, she did believe that he would kill without compunction rather than lose his position as the sixth Earl.

It was so frightening to think about that Farica made herself concentrate on Ivan and the more human and humdrum necessity of providing him with something to eat.

The kitchen was very quiet and the smell of newly washed flagstones mixed with the scent of onions that hung from the rafters of the timbered ceiling.

She went, however, further down the passage to where there was a dairy with its cool marble slabs where there were huge bowls of milk that had already overnight turned to cream.

There was also, she knew, all the food left over from the previous day, besides eggs and butter that had been brought in from the Home Farm.

She found a basket and filled it first with the heavier things, taking slices of ham from a newly cut leg and brawn that the chef had made according to a recipe her father had inherited, which everybody said was more delicious than any brawn they had ever tasted.

There was also an ox tongue that had not yet been cut and the remains of a salmon that had been served hot at dinner the night before.

Farica knew that the salmon had been bought on her father's instructions, as soon as it was caught in the River Avon, which was not very far away.

She felt sure it was a luxury that Ivan must have enjoyed as a boy and he would enjoy it again now.

Having filled one basket she placed into another, a dozen eggs, a pound of golden yellow butter from her father's Jersey herd and a comb of honey from the hives in the kitchen garden.

She then remembered that Ivan would need bread and she recognised as the cooks were not yet down it would be impossible for him to have the freshly baked bread that her father always enjoyed at breakfast.

But there was a small cottage loaf left over from the previous day and she broke it in half and put it on top of her basket.

She was just about to leave when she thought that he would want milk and also coffee or tea.

She found some freshly ground coffee first in the kitchen cupboard and, as time was getting on, she took that and then filled a small jug with milk before she left the house by the back door.

It was rather difficult to carry two quite heavy baskets and a jug of milk, but somehow she managed it, although by the time she reached the doll's house, she seemed to have walked a long way and her arms were aching.

She had been prepared to leave it all outside the door, but Ivan must have seen her through the window for he came out, bending his head to do so and exclaimed,

"How could you come so early and burdened with so much food?"

"I thought you might be hungry," Farica said with a smile.

He had been dressing when she arrived and was wearing only a shirt and his riding breeches, which were not cut as smartly as her father's.

He had, however, already tied his cravat round his neck and she thought that he looked handsome and attractive in a very masculine manner.

Then she blushed because she felt embarrassed to find herself thinking of him in such a way.

But Ivan did not notice.

He had taken the baskets and the jug from her and was carrying them inside the house, remembering to bow his head through the low doorway.

He placed them on the small table where Farica had often given tea parties for her dolls or for her friends.

Because she thought it sensible, her mother had installed a small cooking stove, a replica of the large one in the kitchen of The Priory.

It stood beside the open fireplace and did not have to be used unless she particularly wished to cook.

Needless to say at the time it had been a new toy that Farica had enjoyed enormously. She had cooked all sorts of strange dishes for her friends and had even taken some back to The Priory for her father.

"Now, what is this concoction?" he would ask.

"It's a recipe the chef gave me, Papa, and I made it exactly the way he told me to."

Sometimes it was a success and sometimes a failure, but she thought now that Ivan would at least be able to cook his eggs and coffee on the small stove.

As it was summer, she was sure that he would not mind eating mainly cold food.

He looked at everything she had brought him in astonishment.

"Is this one day's supply," he asked, "or a month's?"

Farica laughed.

"You look as if you need feeding up."

"You insult the nuns who were so kind to me in France."

"I feel that Convent fare is very good for the soul, but not as palatable as you would enjoy if you had the choice."

"I am certainly not complaining at what you have brought me," Ivan said, "and it is very sweet of you to have taken so much trouble."

He spoke in a caressing manner that made her feel as if he was kissing her.

When she realised that he was thinking the same thing, she blushed again.

"I must not stay," she said. "No one must know that I have risen so early."

"I want you to stay with me all day," Ivan smiled. "When you are not here, I feel lost and lonely and, of course, depressed. When you are with me everything is different."

The way he spoke was so beguiling that she looked at him and was lost.

She did not know whether he moved or she did, but the next moment she was in his arms and he was kissing her, not wildly as he had done last night, but gently, possessively and demandingly.

It was as if they belonged to each other and nothing could ever separate them.

"Do you know how beautiful you are?" Ivan said when he could speak. "You are like the sunshine and when you are close to me like this I feel because you believe in me that I can conquer the world."

"That is what you will do," Farica answered, "and the world we know, our world, will be a very much better place because you are ruling it."

Ivan did not answer.

Instead he kissed her until with an effort he set her to one side.

"Go home, my precious," he murmured. "I will light the stove, cook myself some eggs and bless you with every mouthful I eat."

"Shall I stay and cook them for you?" Farica asked him.

It was what she wanted to do, but as she spoke she could not help glancing out of the window to see the sun was beginning to rise in the sky.

"I fear that would be a mistake," Ivan answered seriously. "Should your father learn what is happening, he might inadvertently reveal to my cousin what he feels about his behaviour and that might make him suspicious that I was hiding here on your father's estate. It could also mean that you would be involved."

He drew in his breath and then urged her firmly,

"No! That must not happen. Go back, Farica! I adore you for thinking of me and for everything you are doing, but I must protect you, while God knows I am finding it difficult enough to protect myself."

"I will go because you ask me to," Farica replied, "but I love you – and I shall be praying for you."

She went towards the door and then paused.

"You know I am going driving with your cousin – this afternoon?"

"I had not forgotten," Ivan said in a very different tone of voice. "Must you go? I cannot bear to think of you near that man!"

"I think it wise to allay any suspicions he might have until Hagman can find out what he is planning and where his men who are looking for you have been."

Ivan did not speak and after a moment Farica added,

"Oh, my darling, take care of yourself! If anything should happen to you now – I would not – want to live."

There was a pain in her voice that seemed to echo round the small doll's house.

Then, as Ivan stepped towards her, she ran away from him through the open door and disappeared among the rhododendron bushes.

Not only did she want to conceal the tears that had come to her eyes but also she could not bear to think of him being humiliated like this and forced to hide in what had been her childhood plaything while his cousin Fergus lorded it in The Castle and was served by criminals who were ready to kill on his instructions.

'He is cruel, *cruel*,' Farica said to herself as she walked back to The Priory.

She let herself in through a window that had a defective catch and went up the back stairs, avoiding the housemaids who were already scurrying about the corridors with brooms and dusters in their hands.

She slipped into her bedroom and undressed again and climbed back into bed, trying as she lay down against the soft pillows to think only of Ivan and how much she loved him and to forget all the problems that beset him.

She must have fallen asleep because the next thing she knew was that her maid was pulling back the curtains. The sun was streaming into the room and she realised that it was eight o'clock.

She put on her riding habit to go downstairs and breakfast with her father and afterwards they exercised their horses round the Park and galloped over the flat fields beyond.

As she looked at her father riding one of his magnificent stallions that he had paid a considerable amount of money for, she kept thinking how much Ivan would have enjoyed being with them.

She wondered whether if she told her father the truth he would ask him to join them.

Then she remembered how dangerous that would be while Riggs and perhaps many other hired assassins of the Earl's were searching in the inns, questioning people in the villages and perhaps threatening them if they thought that they were not telling the truth.

"You look worried, my poppet. What is the matter?" Sir Robert asked and Farica realised that they had been riding for some time without her saying a single word.

"I hope you are not worrying about seeing the Earl this afternoon," he went on. "Personally I am looking forward to having tea at The Castle. I particularly want to look at the Conservatory, which I have not seen for quite some time. If you remember, the old Earl had a magnificent collection of orchids. I am sure that some of them should be in flower now, perhaps some I have never seen before."

"I do remember how beautiful they were," Farica smiled.

"You must persuade Fergus to keep adding to the collection, which I believe is unique in the whole of England," Sir Robert pointed out. "It was difficult during the War to obtain new species, but now I am certain that he would find it a great interest and a great joy."

Farica recognised that he was talking as if there was no doubt that she would be Fergus's wife.

She wondered what he would say if she told him that the son-in-law he expected was an imposter and a murderer.

When at two o'clock the Earl arrived with his phaeton to take Farica driving, she could understand how, because he made himself so charming to her father, anyone meeting him socially for the first time would never suspect the depths of his wickedness.

"There are so many things I want to consult you about, Sir Robert," the Earl was saying in an ingratiating tone, which was exactly the way an older man liked to be spoken to by a younger one.

"You are so wise and experienced," he continued, "in country matters, while as you know I have had no opportunity until now to study them. I shall be most grateful for any help you can give me. I hope you will not find it too much of a bother when I bombard you with my problems."

"My dear boy, I am only too willing to do anything I can," Sir Robert replied.

But Farica only felt sick at his hypocrisy.

She had put on one of her prettiest gowns, not to please the Earl whom she hated more every time she saw him, but because she felt it would give her courage.

She had the feeling that they were going to have the usual confrontation as to when she would marry him.

One thing, she told herself as she dressed, was the most important, that he should not have the least suspicion that she was elusive for any other reason except that she felt shy and a little afraid of being married so hastily.

To her surprise, however, when they set off in the phaeton, the Earl did not pay her any compliments or say anything that she might find embarrassing.

Instead he said,

"How delightful your father is. You are very lucky to have a parent who is so fond of you and who you get on so well with."

He gave a sigh and added,

"My father and I never saw eye to eye and, as my mother died when I was young, I was often a very lonely person."

Farica was quite certain that he was saying all this to evoke her sympathy and she replied gently,

"I am sorry for you. As a matter of fact I believe that your uncle would have welcomed you at The Castle, but he always believed that you preferred London."

"London can be a very amusing place for a young man, but it is also very expensive."

"I am sure that is true," Farica agreed.

"Actually," he went on, "I am surprised to find how expensive things can be in the country as well. And that reminds me, I was going to ask you and your father at teatime, but the men arrived just before I was leaving to collect you and I think it would be a mistake if we left them hanging about all afternoon."

"What men?" Farica asked.

"I thought I told you," the Earl answered, "that one of the stained glass windows of the Chapel has been smashed and I have had to employ experts in that particular craft to come to The Castle to mend it."

Farica was surprised because she had never expected that the Earl would be interested in the Chapel.

Although she knew it well and thought it very beautiful, it had not been used for years because the old Earl had always preferred to worship in the village Church where all the Brookes were buried.

"I like to feel them around me," he had said once and she understood what he had meant.

The Chapel was very old and was in a part of The Castle that had never been renovated. And Farica knew that it would be a great tragedy for the stained glass windows, which were at least four hundred years old, to be broken or damaged.

"How did it happen?" she asked.

The Earl shook his head.

"I have no idea, perhaps the wind. As you knew it before it was broken, I thought it would be very helpful if you would tell the men exactly how it should be put together."

"I hope I can," Farica said, "but I have not seen it for some time."

"We will stop now and tell them what to do and then when we come back later we can see if they have done it properly."

As the Earl spoke, he turned his horses into the drive and they drove down the avenue of oak trees until Farica could see the magnificent building just in front of them.

As usual she felt her heart leap at its loveliness.

Then, as she looked up, she saw that the flag which should have been flying because the Earl was in residence, had been forgotten.

Only the flagpole stood silhouetted against the sky and she hoped that it was an omen that Ivan would soon take his place.

The Earl drew up his horses with a flourish outside the front door and she thought, as she had before, that he was not a particularly good driver as her father was and she was certain that Ivan was too.

"Come in and have a look at what is being done," the Earl suggested as they walked up the stone steps and into the hall with its beautiful statues of Greek Gods and pictures of the Brooke ancestors.

As Farica knew, it was quite a long walk to the Chapel along corridors hung with weapons and pictures and decorated with very fine pieces of furniture.

Her father had once said,

"Every time I come to The Castle I realise how impossible it is for one man, however rich he may be, to buy the treasures that can only be collected by a succession of generations."

Farica, knowing that he was feeling envious, had slipped her arm through his as she said,

"You have collected far more beautiful things in your lifetime, Papa, than most men manage to do and I shall be always grateful for your good taste."

Sir Robert had been delighted and kissed her, but she thought now that he had been right.

Only long-established families could, over the centuries, have brought together so many beautiful treasures that were all part of the history of their country.

They reached the Chapel, and as they walked into it, Farica was surprised to see that there were no workmen at any of the windows.

Instead there were great bowls of white flowers on either side of the altar, which was covered with a cloth of white and gold.

There were six lit candles, three on each side of a tall silver cross which she remembered had been made in the reign of King James I and had stood there ever since.

She turned to look questioningly at the Earl who was following her and realised that he was shutting the door behind them.

"Why – where are your workmen?" she began to ask, then saw, moving across the Chancel to stand in front of the altar, a Parson dressed in a white surplice.

"What is – happening?" she enquired nervously.

Then the Earl was standing beside her and he took her hand in his.

"Since you cannot make up your mind," he said, "I have made it up for you. I have brought you here, Farica, to marry you, because I wish to be married and cannot afford any further prevarication."

Although she was incredulous, Farica drew herself up before she replied,

"How dare you do anything so outrageous? Of course I will not marry you in any such circumstances, without Papa, and in such an – underhand manner!"

"You have no choice."

"I have every choice!" Farica retorted. "You cannot force me to say I will marry you – if I do *not* intend to do so."

"Then I shall have to use a little persuasion," the Earl said and there was a nasty note in his voice that alarmed her.

"Nothing you could say or do would persuade me to marry you!"

Her voice was firm and decisive and even though she trembled inside she knew that Ivan would have been proud of her.

It was then that the Earl drew from the pocket of his coat something which she recognised and which she had heard of before.

It was a long thin dagger, something like a stiletto.

It was a replica of the one that he had intended to kill Ivan with when he was in the Convent, but which had in fact murdered an innocent man.

"So you intend to kill me," Farica exclaimed.

"No, of course not," the Earl answered. "You would be quite useless to me dead. But unless you marry me, I intend to mark your face so that no man will ever look at you again except with horror! Only I would be prepared to marry you in such circumstances and you will be grateful to me for doing so!"

The sinister way that he spoke was no less terrifying than his actual threat and Farica gave a little cry of fear and would have stepped backwards if he had not caught hold of her arm.

Then, when she was still shocked at what he intended to do, he pulled her forward until they were standing in front of the Parson.

He was an elderly man with shifty eyes and a shaggy grey beard.

He was holding a Prayer Book in his hands, which were shaking, but Farica did not think it was because he was afraid but because there was a very strong smell of spirits coming from him.

She thought in fact that he had already drunk too much.

Then as she wondered wildly what she could do or how she could escape, the Earl called out sharply,

"Start the Service, you fool!"

The Parson fumbled over the pages of the Prayer Book and then in a slurred voice began,

"*Dearly beloved —* "

"Get to the Service!" the Earl stormed.

Quickly the Parson turned over several more pages of the Prayer Book.

But before he could speak the high silver cross on the altar slipped forward and crashed down on top of the Parson's head.

He collapsed on the floor and, as the Earl let out a shout of anger, a man sprang swiftly from behind the altar and hit him with a resounding punch on the point of the chin.

He seemed to fly through the air and crash down, hitting his head as he did so on the corner of a carved pew and to lie there unconscious.

Then before she could scream, move or even breathe, Farica found herself caught up in Ivan's arms and he was carrying her away towards the door, leaving the two unconscious men behind them.

The door opened just before they reached it and Hagman was outside grinning.

Ivan did not speak, but carried Farica along the passage and out through a door that led into the garden at the back of The Castle.

He crossed the lawn, avoiding the Rose Garden and stepped into the bushes.

He had not gone far before waiting for them tied to a tree was Waterloo.

Ivan put Farica down on the ground and as he did so she gave a little cry and spoke for the first time.

"Oh, Ivan, Ivan – you saved me – I was so – terrified!"

"I knew that you must have been, my darling," he said, "but I had to leave it until the last moment just in case he could escape before I knocked him unconscious."

"It was – so clever of you."

"I must get you away."

Ivan picked her up again as he spoke and put her on the front of his saddle as she had ridden once before.

Then he led the horse through the shrubs until they reached the edge of the garden and beyond where there was an open field.

While they were moving, Farica took off her bonnet to tie it by its ribbons to the saddle.

Ivan then mounted up behind her and she leaned back against him and gave a little sigh of relief and happiness as she did so.

"How could I have guessed – how could I have – imagined," she asked in a low voice, "when he told me a window in the Chapel needed repairing – what he was – really planning?"

"You have to thank Hagman for saving you, my darling one," Ivan replied. "When he arrived to see me this morning after you had left, he told me that two strange things were happening at The Castle that he could find no explanation for."

Ivan kissed Farica's hair before he went on,

"The first was that white flowers had been ordered for the Chapel, which had surprised all the servants as his Lordship had never been to a Service of any kind since he had inherited. And then later a Parson had arrived from London."

"Hagman knew that he was – a Parson?" Farica asked.

"He said he was a strange sort of Parson considering that the moment he stepped into the house before having breakfast he asked for brandy!"

"And Hagman came and told you what was happening?"

"When I heard what he had to say I was frightened," Ivan replied. "I was well aware how much my despicable cousin wanted your money and, because I understand how his devious mind works, I recognised that he was determined to have it."

"How could he think of anything so horrible – so bestial – as to mutilate my face?" Farica muttered.

"He is lucky I did not kill him!" Ivan said. "But I had already decided before I went to the Chapel to save you that the position we are in at the moment cannot continue."

"What are you going – to do?" Farica asked anxiously. "Oh, my darling, be careful. Suppose something should happen – to you?"

"Nothing is going to happen and I will not have you upset," Ivan replied. "I am going to London."

It was the last thing that Farica had expected him to say and it took her a second or so before she could repeat the words,

"To – L-London?"

"When Hagman brought me the newspaper this morning," Ivan explained, "I saw that the Colonel of my Regiment and two of my brother Officers who know me well have returned to England from Paris where they had been in the Army of Occupation. I am going to find them and explain my position and I feel certain that they will help me."

"Oh, Ivan, that is a wonderful idea. If you have soldiers behind you – I shall not feel so afraid."

"There will be a scandal, which is most regrettable," Ivan said in a hard voice, "but something has to be done, as I knew even before that devil terrified you."

Farica turned her face against his shoulder and he kissed her forehead before he said,

"It's all over, my darling, but I do want you to tell your father what has happened."

"You really want me – to tell Papa?"

"But do not mention me," Ivan said quickly. "What I want you to do is to make him realise that you cannot see the Earl in any circumstances, that he is very dangerous and that you must be strongly guarded both in your home and anywhere else you go."

"I am sure if I tell Papa that your cousin tried to marry me by force he will be determined to prevent it from happening again. But how shall I tell him I was saved?"

"Tell him it was one of the servants in The Castle who just placed you outside the door and then hurried away in case he should lose his job."

"I think Papa might believe that – but surely he will think it strange?"

"All that matters," Ivan said, "is that he should make sure that it cannot happen again or anything like it in my absence. I think we can count on Fergus, even if his jaw is not broken, which it probably is, feeling very sorry for himself for the rest of the day and perhaps all day tomorrow. But I intend to be in London by tomorrow evening. After that I will be in charge, at least I hope so!"

"You will be," Farica said prophetically, "and I know, with you directing everything, that I shall be safe."

"With God's help," Ivan said quietly and Farica added very softly,

"I am sure He will help us."

She thought as she spoke of how Ivan had pushed the silver cross down onto the Parson's head, knocking him unconscious before he dealt with his cousin.

She knew it was not only Hagman who had warned them of what was happening, but God, who moving in a mysterious way had first brought them together and then helped them so far in every movement they had made.

"I know you will be successful," she cried. "At the same time I am afraid for you to go away, and you must not travel alone."

"I have thought of that," Ivan replied, "and perhaps I can borrow a horse from someone. I cannot afford to buy one for the moment."

Farica laughed and it was a very tender sound.

"You know perfectly well that you must ride Pegasus and he will be very proud to carry you. Hagman can ride Waterloo and the first thing I am going to find you when I get home is, of course, some money."

She saw Ivan's lips move as if to protest, and she put up her fingers to his mouth to prevent him speaking.

"If after all we have been through," she said, "you are going to pretend that you are proud, I think for the first time I shall be angry, or if not angry with you, offended."

As if he could not help himself, Ivan laughed.

"I suppose considering you have housed me, fed me and kissed me. I am splitting straws, but I can only promise, my sweet, that I will pay you back."

"As a sharp usurer," Farica laughed, "I shall expect one hundred percent for my money – in kisses!"

"You shall have the first one of them now," Ivan said pulling her close to him and at the same time reining in Waterloo.

Farica's lips were ready and waiting for him and he kissed her until everything vanished except the sunshine, which seemed not only to be round them but in them and glowing with a fierce fire.

Then Ivan rode on and a few minutes later they came to the outskirts of The Priory garden.

"Before I tell Papa, I will come back to you with – everything you need," Farica said. "I know he will be working in his study on the plans for the slate mine until it is time for him to go to tea at The Castle. I am therefore going to the stable to collect Pegasus and later I will tell the grooms that I have left him with a friend for the night. Then I will come straight back to you."

"You are quite certain that you will be all right?" Ivan asked and she laughed.

"I don't think that even your appalling cousin will feel strong enough to attack me for an hour or so!"

He held her close against him as if the idea of her being attacked by anyone was terrifying.

Then he said,

"Very well, go quickly, and try not to let anyone ask questions. Remember that Riggs and his accomplices will not yet know what has happened at The Castle."

He saw her slip through the bushes and trees before she reached the stable yard.

There seemed to be no one about and she guessed that the stable boys were exercising the horses while the old groom was taking a rest before getting the carriage ready that would take her father to The Castle.

She went into Pegasus's stall to bridle and saddle him herself and there was still no sign of anyone.

She then entered the house by the door that led only into the garden.

Without being seen she hurried along the passages until she came to the office used by her father's secretary, who she knew was away for three days dealing with her father's affairs in London.

She knew where the keys of the safe were hidden, which contained not only her and her mother's jewellery but also the money that was paid out in wages either weekly or monthly.

Without any difficulty she extracted one hundred pounds and, closing the door of the safe, she put the keys back in their hiding place and returned to the stables.

It was still very quiet except for the movements of the horses in their stalls and she led Pegasus out into the yard, mounted him, and rode away along the twisting path that led first to the gardens and then on towards the doll's house.

Ivan was waiting for her long before she reached him and he lifted her down from the saddle, kissing her as he did so.

"Who saw you?" he asked as he set her down on the ground.

"Nobody," she replied. "And here is your money. But don't forget that you have to pay me for it!"

He kissed her again and slipped the bag that she had carried the money in into his pocket without looking inside it.

Then he led Pegasus up the overgrown narrow path to the doll's house and put him in the small stall that had hitherto held Waterloo, who was tied to a tree.

"He will resent being displaced by Pegasus," Farica smiled.

"He is quite prepared to give way to his elders and betters!" Ivan replied.

He unsaddled Pegasus and took off his bridle, then, as they walked to the front of the doll's house, Ivan said,

"I am sorry, my darling, that I cannot come with you to explain to your father how wonderfully brave you are. I know of no woman who would behave as you have in such horrifying circumstances."

"They were not horrifying – once you had – saved me."

"Nevertheless, you are as brave as you are beautiful! There has never been anyone like you, as you well know."

He kissed her fiercely and demandingly and then he said,

"Therefore, my darling, remember that we have not yet won the battle. This has only been a skirmish, which will put the enemy on their guard."

"I will remember," Farica said solemnly, "and I know that Papa will protect me in every possible way once he learns what has happened."

"Promise me that you also will be very careful. You know now that a cornered rat will fight viciously and that is exactly what Fergus is!"

Farica was frightened, but she did not want Ivan to see it.

Quickly she put her arms around his neck and kissed him and without saying anything more slipped away through the bushes towards The Priory.

She found her father as she expected poring over maps in his study.

"Farica!" he exclaimed. "Why are you here? What has happened?"

"I have something rather – terrible to tell you, Papa," Farica replied.

She threw the bonnet she had carried in her hand since leaving the doll's house on a chair and then sat down beside her father to take his hand in hers.

"I do not want you to be upset about what I have to say, Papa," she began, "although it is in fact – very upsetting."

"What are you talking about and why have you come back alone?"

He sounded slightly perturbed and Farica, holding tightly onto his hand, told him exactly what had happened, only saying that she had no idea who the servant was who had knocked out the Earl and carried her from the Chapel.

"I cannot believe it!" Sir Robert exclaimed in astonishment. "How *dare* the Earl do such a thing! How dare he threaten you in that monstrous manner!"

"Well, I am safe, Papa. The only thing is he may try again."

"Over my dead body will he marry you now!" Sir Robert asserted angrily.

Farica shivered in case what he was saying was unlucky.

Then she said,

"I think, Papa, the kindest way we can look at it is to think that the Earl is a little mad. He needs money so urgently that he is prepared to do anything to get hold of it – but I know that you will save me from it being my money."

"That is certainly true," Sir Robert agreed. "I am only upset, my dearest, that you should have suffered such an unpleasant experience, though one that none of us could possibly have anticipated. When I see that young man, I will tell him exactly what I think of him!"

"No, no, Papa, that will do no good! I think the most dignified thing would be to pretend it has not happened. I do not imagine we shall be seeing the Earl, for some time at any rate."

She paused and then, thinking of what Ivan had said, she added,

"Unless, of course, he wants money so badly that he will try again."

"If you really think that he might try and kidnap you for a second time," Sir Robert said, "that is something I will most certainly prevent!"

He rose from his chair and walked about the study as if only by movement could he relieve his feelings.

Then after a moment he remarked,

"One consolation, if a small one, is that you and I have to be away from here tomorrow, at least for a day, if not longer."

"Away, Papa? But why?"

"After you left a groom arrived from my sister Alice to say that she has had a heart attack and wishes to see us immediately."

"Oh, poor Aunt Alice. How terrible for her," Farica exclaimed.

Her father's sister, Lady Burton, lived about twelve miles away and, although for the moment she had no wish to leave the Priory, just in case she might be of assistance to Ivan, she knew as he was going to London first thing in the morning, it would not matter if she left too.

"We will leave early," Sir Robert suggested, "which means that we should get there at about noon for luncheon. We will then see what we can do for Alice and return in time for dinner."

"I would like that, Papa. I have no wish to stay too long in that uncomfortable house."

"I agree with you," Sir Robert said, "so we have to rise early. And to make sure we do not have any unpleasantness before we leave or during the journey I will take James and Henry with us as outriders."

He paused before he added, almost as if he spoke to himself,

"They are both good shots with a pistol."

"I think that would be wise, Papa, and undoubtedly much safer than if we went alone."

"Safer!" Sir Robert shouted. "It is an outrage that in my own vicinity I have to be afraid of my own neighbours. All I can say is, I would rather see you in your coffin than married to a reprobate like that!"

The way he had changed his mind so completely made Farica want to smile.

At the same time she thought that, if her father knew of the murders the Earl had committed and the way he was hunting the true Earl at this very moment, he would be even more incensed than he was already.

However, she did not say anything, but only rose to her feet and lifted her face to kiss her father on his cheek.

"I love you, Papa, and let's not think or talk about the Earl again. He frightens me."

"The young swine!" Sir Robert growled.

But he said no more.

CHAPTER SEVEN

Farica awoke early, but not early enough to enable her to slip away and see Ivan without her absence being noticed.

She dearly wanted to do so, but she knew that it would be a great mistake if her father discovered at this particular moment that Ivan was alive and hiding in the doll's house.

She was well aware without his saying so that what Ivan wanted was to be able to meet her father as himself and not as a fugitive from one of his own relatives.

She therefore got up and dressed and by the time she was ready in a pretty gown with a bonnet and a shawl to match in which she was to travel, it was time for breakfast.

She was not surprised to find that her father was already downstairs, because he was always an early riser.

She had a feeling that he was still so interested in his plans for the slate mine that he had been taking a last look at them before he had to leave The Priory for the day.

He ate a large breakfast as usual in the small dining room, and Farica, as she helped herself, was hoping that Ivan was sensible enough to eat plenty of breakfast before he set out on what she was well aware would be an arduous ride to London.

He would have to stay one night on the way, if only to give the horses a rest.

It was usual when her father made the trip for him to stay for two nights on the way if possible with friends.

Then Farica began to worry in case Ivan was seen and recognised in the village and Riggs or some others of the Earl's assassins followed and killed him while he was unprotected at some wayside inn.

But she told herself she was being faint-hearted. Ivan had said she was brave and that was what she must be.

Her father, having finished his breakfast, then said,

"The sooner we are off the better. I expect when we reach your aunt's house we shall find that she is fully recovered and cannot imagine why we are making such a fuss over her."

Farica laughed because it sounded so like her Aunt Alice.

She collected her gloves and a small handbag that contained a handkerchief and waited for her father while a footman brought him his tall hat and riding gloves.

"You look very smart today, Papa," Farica said. "And I do like your buttonhole."

Sir Robert glanced down at it and smiled.

It was a small orchid from his greenhouse and she knew without his saying anything that he was regretting that the collection of orchids at The Castle that he had admired so much would now be out of his reach.

They climbed into the phaeton which was waiting for them, which was not as up to date or smart as the one that the Earl had taken her driving in yesterday afternoon.

But it was well sprung and was drawn by a perfectly matched team of four horses.

Then the young groom, having released the horses' heads, jumped up into the small seat behind them and they started off down the drive.

Because it was so early it was cool and the sun had little heat in it, but Farica suspected that during the day it would grow warmer and she hoped that Ivan would not be uncomfortably hot on the long ride ahead of him.

They turned out of the gates along the narrow lane, its hedges covered in honeysuckle that led through the small village and past *The Fox and Goose* where Abe tended his animals and from there to the high road.

Without really meaning to, Farica looked about her searching for a sign of Riggs or his confederates who would be, she was sure, still visiting all the small villages in the neighbourhood.

Then, as they passed the duck pond and came to the village green with the inn on their left, she gave a little gasp.

Outside *The Fox and Goose* was a large crowd of people.

In fact it appeared as if the whole village was there, apart from some women and children who were still running across the grass to where the others were congregated.

"What has – happened, Papa?" Farica asked in a frightened voice.

"I have no idea," Sir Robert replied, "but I shall certainly go and see."

He drove his horses across the grass towards the inn.

Then, as they reached it, Farica gave a stifled scream of horror.

Standing just outside the door of the inn was Abe with Riggs on one side of him and a burly-looking man rather like him on the other.

Each of them was holding a heavy stick in one hand and with the other held Abe prisoner by his arms.

All around them, shouting and expostulating, were the people of the village who had obviously come straight from where they were working.

Some of the men were carrying pitchforks or spades, others had sickles or scythes, and there were woodcutters holding their axes and saws.

They were all shouting at once, making an incoherent babble, which made it impossible to understand what they were saying.

It was quite obvious, however, that they were protesting against something and Farica was sure that it was what the two men were doing to Abe.

Then, as her father drew in his horses, she saw that at the edge of the crowd, having obviously just dismounted from his horse, was the Earl.

He had his back to them, but the mere sight of him was enough to make Farica feel as if every nerve in her body became tense.

Instinctively she moved a little closer to her father and put her hand on his knee.

"What the devil is going on?" Sir Robert asked in an irritated tone.

At that moment Riggs's voice rang out above the yells of the crowd,

"'E says, my Lord, 'e don't know nothin'!"

Riggs was obviously speaking to the Earl and just for a moment the people around him were silent as if they wished to hear the answer.

"Then beat it out of him!" the Earl replied and he seemed to snarl the words.

It was then, as the two men raised their sticks to strike old Abe and Farica gave a scream of protest, that an axe flew from the back of the crowd.

No one knew who threw it, but it landed on the base of the Earl's head, knocked off his high hat and buried itself in his neck.

Without a murmur he fell forward onto the ground.

Suddenly the crowd lost control and as he lay there, with his horse rearing in terror, forks and pickaxes were driven into his body, while Riggs, about to strike Abe, had half his leg slashed away by a scythe and his accomplice was knocked unconscious with a spade.

For a moment there was nothing but turmoil and the noise was as if a number of wild animals had been let loose on their prey.

Then, as Farica sat frozen with horror, her hands pressed instinctively against her breast, round the corner of the inn came Ivan riding Pegasus.

With him was Hagman on Waterloo.

Farica drew in her breath.

She saw Ivan take in what had happened, while the crowd, as if they were aware of his presence, were suddenly afraid and moved back a few steps.

Ivan could see the body of the Earl pinioned to the ground with forks, the blood running from the axe that had first felled him seeping crimson over his coat.

His two henchmen, Riggs and the other man, lay prostrate on the ground on either side of Abe, who had not moved.

Riggs groaned as the blood ran down his leg onto the dusty ground, while the other man was still and silent.

For a few seconds, although it seemed to Farica far longer because she could not move or think, Ivan stared at the spectacle in front of him.

Then he dismounted Pegasus, handed the reins to the nearest boy and moved through the crowd that was suddenly hushed and silent as if apprehensive over what they had done.

He sprang onto a heavy oak table where the old folk sat in the evening outside the inn drinking ale or cider.

Somehow to Farica he looked different until she realised that it was because for the first time she saw him dressed as a gentleman in the height of fashion.

She knew that Hagman must have brought him clothes from The Castle.

For a few moments he stood on the table looking at the crowd below him.

Then he began,

"My people, by the mercy of God, after I was left for dead at the Battle of Waterloo, I am now able to return to you and take my rightful place, now that my father is dead, as the sixth Earl of Lydbrooke!"

There was an audible gasp and then complete silence as if everybody listening held their breath and then Ivan continued,

"I am sure, although I have been away for many years, some of you will remember me, although, as you can see, I was wounded on the field of battle. I understand that in my absence a great many things have changed since my father's death, which is not to my liking. I want your help and that means from every one of you, to restore The Castle and the estate exactly as it was in my father's and grandfather's time. This means that I am asking everybody who has been dismissed to return immediately."

He paused to look round him at the mesmerised crowd and then went on,

"I want the Prospers and the Bradshaws to take over the farms again that they looked after in the past. The same applies to anybody who was employed in the gardens or on the land. There will be problems, of course there will be, but I shall be here and I am quite certain that you and I can solve them all together."

He smiled before adding,

"All I want now is to thank God for bringing me home and for making sure that together, we can make The Castle and the estate as fine and beautiful as it has been in the past."

As Ivan finished speaking, there was first a gasp and then they were cheering, cheering him wildly and spontaneously, waving their tools, their caps and their handkerchiefs in the air.

He had spoken with such sincerity that Farica could hardly see him through her tears.

Now she was aware that many of the village women were crying openly, while the men surged forward to shake him by the hand and tell him over and over again how glad they were to see him back.

It was then that Sir Robert, looking down at Farica and seeing the tears on her cheeks, suggested,

"I think, my dearest, we should leave the Hero of the Day to his Hour of Triumph. There will be plenty of time for us to congratulate him later."

He did not wait for her answer, but lifted the reins and drove on.

Only as they went did Farica look back to have a last glimpse of Ivan bending down from the table to shake hands with the people who were still wildly cheering him.

*

After they had seen Sir Robert's sister and found, as he had expected, that she had recovered from her heart attack and was quite surprised that they should have taken the trouble to drive over to see her, Farica realised that her father had deliberately not talked about the extraordinary scene that they had just witnessed in the village.

She had been glad in a way because it had been a tremendous shock first to realise what Riggs had intended to do to Abe and then to see the Earl killed in front of her.

She recognised that it was what he deserved. At the same time the sight of the axe buried in his neck and the villagers striking him as he lay on the ground seemed like something out of a nightmare.

But it made, she realised, the situation very much easier for Ivan.

Now there was no need for him to go to London or to involve force against his own cousin.

She was quite certain that, as everybody would want to return to what they considered normal, The Castle in a very few days, perhaps even hours, would be itself again.

She felt, however, tearful and a little faint as her father had driven her away from *The Fox and Goose*.

Although her heart was singing because everything had come right, she felt that it was something that when it happened had been so horrible that she did not want to talk or even think about it.

It was only as they started homewards at about two o'clock that she realised how tactful her father had been and knew that it was because he loved her.

They had a closeness that was very precious.

But, as they drove down the drive and out through the iron gates and set off towards the main road to make for home, Sir Robert said quietly,

"I think, my dearest, I am not mistaken in thinking that you have kept something from me."

Farica gave him a quick glance and he explained,

"I noticed that the new Earl was riding Pegasus and, as I cannot believe that he stole him from my stables, I can only conclude that you lent him your horse."

Farica drew in her breath.

"You are quite right, Papa – I did lend Pegasus to him. I have a great – deal to tell you."

"Why did you not confide in me before?" Sir Robert asked and she knew that he was hurt by her secrecy.

"The answer to that is quite simple, Papa. Ivan warned me that, if I told you what I had discovered quite by chance, I would be signing your death warrant!"

Sir Robert looked startled and then, as Farica unfolded the strange story, which seemed almost too fantastic to be true, he listened attentively without making any comment until she had finished.

She spoke in a very low voice because she did not wish the groom behind them to overhear what they were saying.

In fact it would have been an impossibility because they were travelling very fast and the open hood of the phaeton was between them and the seat behind.

Only when she had told her father how Ivan had been on his way to London to see his Colonel and ask for Military aid did Sir Robert say approvingly,

"That was a sensible thing to do. Even so it would have caused a great deal of talk and gossip and Fergus Brooke might have managed to add another crime to his already long list."

There was a note of anger in her father's voice that Farica did not miss and she said,

"He was very clever and plausible, Papa. You could not possibly have known how despicable and wicked he really was!"

"If I had been using my senses and my instinct properly," Sir Robert answered sharply, "I should have guessed."

He paused before he added,

"You must forgive me, my dearest, because I was blinded by my ambitions for you and I can only thank God who in His mercy saved you from being married to a man like that."

Her father did not press her to say any more about her relationship with Ivan than she had already told him.

But she had the feeling that he already suspected what they felt for each other.

It was late in the afternoon when they passed through the village and everything seemed quiet.

There was no sign of the tumult that had taken place in the morning.

Farica guessed that the dead body of the Earl would have been taken to the family Church, which

~169~

was about a mile down the road outside the gates of The Castle.

She did not, however, ask any questions and her father hurried on as if he was anxious to be back at The Priory.

'Tomorrow,' Farica thought, 'I must go to see old Abe and make certain that he is none the worse for what has happened here today.'

The mellow red brick walls and the diamond-paned windows of The Priory looked very beautiful and welcoming and when she walked in, knowing from the expression on the butler's face that he was longing to tell them what had happened, she quickly ran up to her room.

Her maid was waiting for her and, after she had bathed and changed into an evening gown, the maid said,

"I daresay you've 'eard already, miss, the terrible things as 'ave 'appened in the village this mornin'!"

"Yes, I know all about it, thank you, Emily," Farica replied, "but I don't want to talk about it."

She hurried downstairs, expecting to find her father waiting for her in the drawing room. To her surprise there was a man standing by the mantelpiece and, as he turned round, she gave a little cry of sheer happiness.

It was Ivan.

Without thinking or asking questions she just ran down the room to fling herself into his arms.

He kissed her wildly and passionately until he at last raised his head to say,

"My sweet. My darling. It is all due to you and, because I had to see you, I have come here to ask if I may have dinner tonight with my nearest and most precious neighbour."

"Are you all right? There will be no more – trouble?"

The tears were back in her eyes and Ivan kissed them before his lips found hers once again.

Only when she felt that they were flying in the sky and that there was no need for explanations or for her to feel anything except the beat of Ivan's heart did he say,

"I love you! God, how I love you! I have come to ask your father if I may marry you immediately. I cannot do all there is to do without you."

It was impossible for Farica to answer because his lips were holding her captive and they only moved apart when the door opened and Sir Robert came into the room.

*

The crowd of villagers outside the Church showered the bridal couple with flower petals of every sort as they came out into glorious sunshine.

The diamonds in Farica's tiara glittered no more brightly than her eyes.

They stopped for a moment after they had passed through the lychgate for her to pat Pegasus, who was waiting for them with a wreath of flowers round his neck and his saddle decorated in the same way.

Ivan patted him too and then after he had helped Farica into the open carriage, which was also decorated with flowers, there was another shower of petals that made Pegasus toss his head and rear to show his dislike of such ostentation before he followed in the bridal procession to The Castle.

"I realise, Sir Robert," Ivan had said, "that you expect Farica to be married from your own house, but I want to ask you to be generous and allow the marriage festivities to take place at The Castle."

Sir Robert had looked surprised and Ivan went on,

"My people have suffered more than I can put into words during the months that Fergus usurped my position and was in control. It is hard to believe that anyone could have been so cruel as to send away the old servants without proper pensions, without cottages and with no more than twenty-four hours' notice."

He saw that Sir Robert understood what he was saying and carried on,

"They are, of course, very voluble about their suffering and their fears and I am thinking not only of them but of Farica and myself when I want to give them something else to talk about."

Sir Robert laughed.

"And that, you think, should be your Wedding!"

"They will be thrilled by it and I am certain that it will make them forget their unhappiness more quickly than anything else," Ivan said simply.

Sir Robert put his hand on Ivan's shoulder.

"You are a very wise young man and, of course, I understand. But I hope my own people, who have known Farica for so many years, will be invited to the festivities too."

"You need not doubt that," Ivan assured him. "I am having two huge marquees erected on the lawns and the presents, although there will not be many, will be shown in the ballroom of The Castle. I think we must also include a display of fireworks, besides the usual barrels of ale and kegs of cider and naturally the roasting of a whole ox which is traditional."

His eyes were twinkling as he spoke and Sir Robert laughed again.

"It will certainly be something to remember," he said.

"That is exactly what I am hoping," Ivan agreed.

To Farica it was as if every Fairytale she had ever read had come true.

It was impossible to feel happier than she was and she knew that every time Ivan kissed her, in fact every time they saw each other, she loved him more and she knew that he felt the same.

"You know where we really ought to spend our honeymoon?" he said teasingly.

"Where?" she asked.

"In the doll's house!" he replied.

"I think that would be a little too cramped," Farica protested, "but where are we going?"

"The answer to that is quite simple. Nowhere!"

She looked at him in surprise and he said,

"I think we have both passed through too many traumatic and emotional experiences to want to travel for any distance. What we want is the security of being at home, at least I know I do."

Then, as if he thought that she might be disappointed, he said quickly,

"If you really want to go to London or to a house I own in Newmarket, we will go there, but I thought, my precious, it would be wonderful for us to stay at home and start doing the million things that need doing in The Castle and which no one can do but ourselves."

"That is what I would like too," Farica sighed.

"Do you really mean that?"

"Of course I mean it. The only thing that really matters is that I shall be with you."

"I will not tell you about my plans. They are to be secret until our Wedding Day," Ivan said softly.

He smiled at her and then, as he put his arms around her, she ceased to think of anything but the wild sensations of excitement he aroused within her just because he was touching her.

Now, driving up to The Castle in the sunshine and holding tightly onto Ivan's hand, Farica thought that their Wedding, which had taken place within four days of his claiming his rightful place, was exactly what she wanted. And yet she had never thought to put it into words.

Because they were strictly speaking in mourning, although for a man who was evil and wicked, no outsiders, not even their close relatives, were invited to the Wedding.

The Church was filled with the senior servants from The Castle and The Priory, the farmers, the Head Gardeners and their wives and the Head Gamekeepers.

They sat proudly, all wearing their best, in the pews that on other occasions had held the most distinguished personages in the land and in the very front sat Abe and Hagman.

Because there was no time to buy a new Wedding dress, Farica wore one of the beautiful gowns that her father had bought for her to wear in London on an occasion that had never taken place.

She wore a lace veil that had been in the Brooke family for generations, a tiara that the Earl's mother had worn on her Wedding Day and a necklace of diamonds that was part of the Brooke collection and so beautiful that Farica felt that she had never even imagined anything to equal it.

"You look like a Fairy Princess, my darling," Ivan said when for a moment there was no cheering at the side of the road and no flower petals falling against their cheeks.

"I want to look as beautiful as I can for you."

"Could you be anything else?" he asked. "When I first saw you, I thought that you were the most beautiful woman I had ever seen in my life and now I know that no Countess of Lydbrooke has ever equalled your loveliness. In fact I intend to have you painted a thousand times so that there is a portrait of you in every room in the house!"

Farica laughed before she protested,

"People would think me very conceited if I allowed you to do anything of the sort. What I want to make sure of is that you look at me and at no other woman."

"There is no other woman except you in the whole world," Ivan said and she knew from the deep passionate note in his voice how much he wanted her.

There were more people waiting for them at The Castle, many of them running behind them up the drive or across the fields to be there as quickly as possible.

They had gone first into the house, but there was no long line of guests to shake hands with.

Instead they admired the Wedding presents, which had been arranged in the ballroom, although there were not many of them as so few people knew about the intended marriage.

Then they went into the marquees to cut a Wedding cake in each one and for Ivan to make a speech.

It all took time, until finally Sir Robert said 'goodbye' and drove back to The Priory, the lanterns had been lit in the marquees and the last firework had sizzled out over the lake illuminating the excited faces of the village children who were seeing fireworks for the first time.

It was all very simple and very happy and Farica asked Ivan,

"What do we do now?"

"First we have something to eat and one of my surprises is where it will take place."

Farica had expected that they would be sleeping in the great Master Bedroom where all the Earls of Lydbrooke had slept and that her room would be the one next door, which had not been changed since Ivan's mother had died.

But instead Ivan took her to another part of The Castle and into some rooms that she had never seen before, but which as she entered them were fragrant with the scent of flowers.

She looked around and realised that the orchids had been brought in from the Conservatory to decorate the whole room.

They made it so beautiful that she gave a little gasp and Ivan explained,

"I am having the rooms that we should by tradition use redecorated and in the meantime, my darling, I thought you would be happier here. These are the rooms I used myself when I was a boy before I went to the War, but which I have learnt from the servants have never been used since."

Farica knew that in a subtle way he was telling her that he did not wish her to sleep in any room that had been contaminated by Fergus and that when the Master Bedrooms had been redecorated all trace of him would have disappeared.

She thought that no one could be more perceptive than Ivan and she moved closer to him.

He put his arm around her as he went on,

"Come, my precious one, and see where we shall sleep tonight."

He opened the door into the next room and she knew that he must have worked at an incredible speed to turn what she was sure had been quite an ordinary bedroom into a bower worthy of any Goddess.

There was a huge bed, which she suspected came from another part of The Castle with a gold corolla hung from the ceiling from which fell curtains exactly the colour of her eyes.

But it was difficult to see anything else because again there were flowers, white orchids, white lilacs and white roses, hanging in garlands on the walls and filling the fireplace, because it was too hot to need a fire.

Flowers also flanked on either side of the bed, making it a resting place for Aphrodite herself.

"It's lovely! Perfectly lovely," Farica exclaimed. "Thank you, darling, for thinking of it."

She lifted her lips to his and he kissed her gently. And then drew her back into the sitting room.

Already the servants were bringing in their supper and, as they sat down at the table, Ivan lifted his glass of champagne.

"To my wife," he toasted softly, "who has guided, helped and inspired me ever since I first met her."

Farica looked across the table at her husband and said in a whisper,

"To the most wonderful man in the whole world."

She knew what she said excited Ivan, but the servants were bringing in the food on silver dishes and they could only behave conventionally until supper was finished.

When it was over, as if on Ivan's instructions, the footmen lifted up the whole table and carried it from the sitting room instead of clearing it, which would have taken more time.

When the door was finally closed behind them, Ivan put his arms around Farica and drew her to the window.

The rooms they were in looked over the back of The Castle so that there was no sound to disturb them and no lights from the marquees to intrude on the quiet beauty of the garden.

Instead there was a fountain throwing its water iridescent towards the stars and there was the scent of honeysuckle and wild rose coming in through the open window.

"This is what I dreamt about all those years when I was fighting first in the Peninsula and then in France," Ivan said. "I used to imagine myself back here, looking out as we are doing now, before I went to bed."

Farica put her cheek in a loving gesture against his as he went on,

"In my dreams there was always somebody here with me, for I was never alone. I know now, my darling, that somebody was *you*!"

"Do you really – believe we have – met before – in other lives?" Farica asked.

"Of course we have," he answered. "And we have been journeying towards each other, perhaps for thousands of years. Now that we have found what we have been seeking, we shall be together for all eEernity."

"That is – what I want to – believe."

"It is what I do believe," Ivan declared. "No one, except somebody as perfect as you, my precious darling, could have loved me as a hunted man, possessing nothing but a horse, a pistol and a few sovereigns."

Farica laughed and it seemed to take away the solemnity of the way that Ivan had spoken.

"But you were still very proud," she said softly. "So proud that I was afraid you would not accept anything from me, even the food, which was very heavy when I carried it from the dairy up to the doll's house."

Ivan sighed.

"I have never in my life envisaged marrying a woman for her money or having a wife who is richer than I am myself."

"Does it matter?" Farica asked quickly.

"I was just going to tell you," he answered, "that one of the lessons you have taught me is that money is of no importance whatsoever besides love."

"Do you really mean that? You promise you will not – resent my having such a – large fortune?"

"It belongs to both of us now, my darling," he said quietly, "just as The Castle is yours, my people are your people and we share everything we possess, so that it is impossible to know where your half starts and mine begins."

Farica gave a little cry.

"Oh, Ivan darling, that is what I want you to feel, and I have been so afraid that – you might resent – "

He stopped what she was going to say with his lips.

Only when he had kissed her so that her heart was beating violently against his did he say,

"There is one way, my lovely wife, that I can prove to you once and for all time that there is no question of *my* possessions or *yours*."

"How can – you do – that?"

It was difficult to understand what he was saying because of the rapture that he had evoked within her so that she wanted him to kiss her and go on kissing her.

His arms tightened and to her surprise he led her from the sitting room into the bedroom where, while they were having supper together, everything had been laid ready for them.

The bed had been turned down and there were just two lit candles one on either side of the bed.

Ivan held her very close against him, but he did not kiss her.

Instead he pulled the pins from her hair so that it fell over her shoulders and he thought again, as he had the first time he had seen her, that it was the colour of the copper beech trees with the sun tipping the leaves with gold.

Then, as she looked up at him, he undid her gown at the back and she felt it fall to the floor like the soft movement of the wind in the trees.

She felt herself thrill and would have hidden her face against him because she felt shy.

But Ivan picked her up in his arms and, carrying her to the bed, laid her down against the pillows.

It was only a few seconds before he joined her and, as she felt him close against her, her heart was beating frantically.

Her love seemed to rise within her so overwhelmingly that she felt as if he carried her along with the swiftness and force of a tidal wave and she did not know where she was going.

"I – love you!" she said and she saw that his lips were very close to hers.

"And I love you, my precious darling," he breathed. "This is the moment when I prove to you that we are no longer two individuals but one person. What is yours is mine and what is mine is yours. What is more, my wonderful perfect darling, you are completely mine and I will never lose you."

As he spoke, his lips first found hers and then he was kissing her wildly, her eyes, her cheeks, the softness of her neck until Farica stirred.

Now she knew that the ecstasy he was feeling was the same ecstasy that she felt.

Gently he kissed the softness of her breasts and she could feel his heart beating against hers.

Never had she known such rapture or such excitement, which made her feel as wild as the wind and yet burning with the heat of the sun.

"I love you, Ivan!" she cried. "I love you – please love me – so that I belong to you completely!"

"You are mine," Ivan asserted, "*mine*! And, my beloved little wife, nothing shall ever divide us."

Then, as he made Farica his, she understood why he had said that they were now one person.

They were one and there was only the scent of the flowers, the sound of the angels and the stars looking down on them from the sky above to tell them that they had one heart, one soul, one body and their great love came from one God.

OTHER BOOKS IN THIS SERIES

The Barbara Cartland Eternal Collection is the unique opportunity to collect all five hundred of the timeless beautiful romantic novels written by the world's most celebrated and enduring romantic author.

Named the Eternal Collection because Barbara's inspiring stories of pure love, just the same as love itself, the books will be published on the internet at the rate of four titles per month until all five hundred are available.

The Eternal Collection, classic pure romance available worldwide for all time.

1. Elizabethan Lover
2. The Little Pretender
3. A Ghost in Monte Carlo
4. A Duel of Hearts
5. The Saint and the Sinner
6. The Penniless Peer
7. The Proud Princess
8. The Dare-Devil Duke
9. Diona and a Dalmatian
10. A Shaft of Sunlight
11. Lies for Love
12. Love and Lucia
13. Love and the Loathsome Leopard
14. Beauty or Brains
15. The Temptation of Torilla
16. The Goddess and the Gaiety Girl
17. Fragrant Flower
18. Look, Listen and Love
19. The Duke and the Preacher's Daughter
20. A Kiss For The King
21. The Mysterious Maid-Servant
22. Lucky Logan Finds Love
23. The Wings of Ecstasy
24. Mission to Monte Carlo
25. Revenge of the Heart
26. The Unbreakable Spell
27. Never Laugh at Love
28. Bride to a Brigand
29. Lucifer and the Angel
30. Journey to a Star
31. Solita and the Spies
32. The Chieftain without a Heart
33. No Escape from Love
34. Dollars for the Duke
35. Pure and Untouched
36. Secrets
37. Fire in the Blood
38. Love, Lies and Marriage
39. The Ghost who fell in love
40. Hungry for Love
41. The wild cry of love

42. The blue eyed witch
43. The Punishment of a Vixen
44. The Secret of the Glen
45. Bride to The King
46. For All Eternity
47. A King in Love
48. A Marriage Made in Heaven
49. Who Can Deny Love?
50. Riding to The Moon
51. Wish for Love
52. Dancing on a Rainbow
53. Gypsy Magic
54. Love in the Clouds
55. Count the Stars
56. White Lilac
57. Too Precious to Lose
58. The Devil Defeated
59. An Angel Runs Away
60. The Duchess Disappeared
61. The Pretty Horse-breakers
62. The Prisoner of Love
63. Ola and the Sea Wolf
64. The Castle made for Love
65. A Heart is Stolen
66. The Love Pirate
67. As Eagles Fly
68. The Magic of Love
69. Love Leaves at Midnight
70. A Witch's Spell
71. Love Comes West
72. The Impetuous Duchess
73. A Tangled Web
74. Love Lifts the Curse
75. Saved By A Saint
76. Love is Dangerous
77. The Poor Governess
78. The Peril and the Prince
79. A Very Unusual Wife
80. Say Yes Samantha
81. Punished with love
82. A Royal Rebuke
83. The Husband Hunters
84. Signpost To Love
85. Love Forbidden
86. Gift of the Gods
87. The Outrageous Lady
88. The Slaves of Love
89. The Disgraceful Duke
90. The Unwanted Wedding
91. Lord Ravenscar's Revenge
92. From Hate to Love
93. A Very Naughty Angel
94. The Innocent Imposter
95. A Rebel Princess
96. A Wish Come True
97. Haunted
98. Passions In The Sand
99. Little White Doves of Love
100. A Portrait of Love
101. The Enchanted Waltz
102. Alone and Afraid
103. The Call of the Highlands
104. The Glittering Lights
105. An Angel in Hell
106. Only a Dream
107. A Nightingale Sang
108. Pride and the Poor Princess
109. Stars in my Heart
110. The Fire of Love
111. A Dream from the Night
112. Sweet Enchantress
113. The Kiss of the Devil
114. Fascination in France
115. Love Runs in
116. Lost Enchantment
117. Love is Innocent
118. The Love Trap
119. No Darkness for Love
120. Kiss from a Stranger
121. The Flame Is Love
122. A Touch Of Love
123. The Dangerous Dandy
124. In Love In Lucca

125. The Karma of Love
126. Magic from the Heart
127. Paradise Found
128. Only Love
129. A Duel with Destiny
130. The Heart of the Clan
131. The Ruthless Rake
132. Revenge Is Sweet
133. Fire on the Snow
134. A Revolution of Love
135. Love at the Helm
136. Listen to Love
137. Love Casts out Fear
138. The Devilish Deception
139. Riding in the Sky
140. The Wonderful Dream
141. This Time it's Love
142. The River of Love
143. A Gentleman in Love
144. The Island of Love
145. Miracle for a Madonna
146. The Storms of Love
147. The Prince and the Pekingese
148. The Golden Cage
149. Theresa and a Tiger
150. The Goddess of Love
151. Alone in Paris
152. The Earl Rings a Belle
153. The Runaway Heart
154. From Hell to Heaven
155. Love in the Ruins
156. Crowned with Love
157. Love is a Maze
158. Hidden by Love
159. Love Is The Key
160. A Miracle In Music
161. The Race For Love
162. Call of The Heart
163. The Curse of the Clan
164. Saved by Love
165. The Tears of Love
166. Winged Magic
167. Born of Love
168. Love Holds the Cards
169. A Chieftain Finds Love
170. The Horizons of Love
171. The Marquis Wins
172. A Duke in Danger
173. Warned by a Ghost
174. Forced to Marry
175. Sweet Adventure
176. Love is a Gamble
177. Love on the Wind
178. Looking for Love
179. Love is the Enemy
180. The Passion and the Flower
181. The Reluctant Bride
182. Safe in Paradise
183. The Temple of Love
184. Love at First Sight
185. The Scots Never Forget
186. The Golden Gondola
187. No Time for Love
188. Love in the Moon
189. A Hazard of Hearts
190. Just Fate
191. The Kiss of Paris
192. Little Tongues of Fire
193. Love under Fire
194. The Magnificent Marriage
195. Moon over Eden
196. The Dream and The Glory
197. A Victory for Love
198. A Princess in Distress
199. A Gamble with Hearts
200. Love strikes a Devil